T0367498

THE
BRIBE

Oskar Klausenstock

iUniverse LLC
Bloomington

THE BRIBE

iUniverse books may be ordered through booksellers or by contacting:

iUniverse
1663 Liberty Drive
Bloomington, IN 47403
www.iuniverse.com
1-800-Authors (1-800-288-4677)

ISBN: 978-1-4917-0914-6 (sc)
ISBN: 978-1-4917-0915-3 (hc)
ISBN: 978-1-4917-0916-0 (e)

Library of Congress Control Number: 2013917161

Printed in the United States of America.

iUniverse rev. date: 9/23/2013

CHAPTER

1

Morning sunlight streams through my window, left partly open to air the mustiness of my room. The autumn breeze billows the flimsy curtains, and I can hear the arrival of the Long Island commuter bus. It comes to a full halt just around the corner and does so with the squealing of breaks, the door opening with a hiss, the clattering of footsteps on the sidewalk, and the familiar, high-pitched voice saying to the driver, "Bye, Damon. See you later." It is my daily wake-up call. The morning shift at the Rehabilitation Center has arrived. Each morning, within minutes of the bus stopping, a soft knock on my door announces the arrival of Miss Hedberg. Dressed in a white smock, her cheeks flushed, a broad smile on her round face, she enters my room trailing a gust of fresh air and the scent of lavender.

"Ja, ja, we are doing well, real well, Mr. Klein," she says, and it sounds like a Swedish lullaby. "Just a few more sessions with the walker, and before you know it, we'll be up again and jogging down the garden path."

Heavy-footed, sleeves rolled up, she helps me into the wheelchair. Physical Therapy, says the sign on the door leading to a large room, the walls an antiseptic white, the many mirrors reflecting other mirrors into infinity. Exercise equipment lines the walls, and this too is multiplied to look like banks of armor arranged in rows.

"Bend your knee, ja, ja. Now flex your arm. Make a fist, Mr. Klein." She speaks softly. "Just a little more. Ja, ja, that is good, Mr. Klein. Now let's try it on the left side. No, no." She shakes her head. "You mustn't look at me like that. I know we can do it. There, you see?"

She bends and stretches my left arm at the elbow; only a flicker of life resides there. "Now, now, Mr. Klein, don't let me stretch it. Hold it. Just try and fight me. There, you see? It's coming back now. You've got a lot more muscle power than you think."

Miss Ulrica Hedberg—ample bosom, broad shoulders, powerful arms, hair the color of ripe wheat—projects light and strength. A Viking helmet, a breastplate, and she'd be Helga, the buxom wife of Hagar the Horrible, the no-nonsense, eminently practical keeper of the Viking hearth. I disliked her at first, when she began to manipulate my extremities with the proficiency of a mechanic to whom I was no more than a number of defective parts in need of repair. I didn't like her, for she, more than anyone, highlighted the extent of my defectiveness. In time though, I began to appreciate her direct manner that contained no trace of pity, that old enemy of mine, one I'm quick to detect within myself and within others, even if all too often imagined.

I would watch her bending my flail and nearly helpless arm, listen to her assuring voice, her promise that it was bound to become stronger any day now, knowing it was a lie, yet wanting to believe her with the faith of a child wanting to believe in magic.

Going back to my room, the corridor always seems longer. I'm alone now and tired. The tiredness seems to reside somewhere in my head; it is only half past nine in the morning. The room is small and compact, though large enough that I don't bump my wheelchair into things or have to back up incessantly to get to the window or door. It contains a bed, a desk near the window, two chairs, including a comfortable one with armrests, a dresser, and a throw rug—a cheap one, the edges frayed and linty. Damn thing forever gets caught in the wheels. And there's that painting on the wall, right above the foot of my bed. A bucolic scene of a pine forest at the edge of a lake. Cheap, probably done by the numbers and sold in the nickel and dime stores. The forest in that painting is still and lifeless. A naked sky, not a bird in flight or on a branch, and the water crystal as if it had turned to ice. As if life had fled from there, as if nature too had suffered from a stroke and became paralyzed.

3

Strange and disturbing, those thoughts of mine as I sit alone in my wheelchair near the single window looking down into the garden. Not much out there to gaze at this time of the year, autumn wilt having blanched the summer colors of the flowerbeds. A milky sky, a few benches along a gravel path leading toward a semicircle of other buildings—pavilions, they call them—and a few trees, an elm, a maple, and some whose names I never knew. Some have already shed their leaves, and the small fountain near the center is no longer spouting water, the basin rust-stained and cluttered with wilted leaves.

"Rest," the doctor said. "Rest and sleep." But I'm awake, listening to the monotone cooing of the pigeons roosting beneath the eaves above my window, trying to decipher their mysterious language. And there is that never-changing, drip, drip, drip of a leaky faucet and the incessant whisper coming from the toilet bowl. I'm an old man surrounded by things defective. Things around me, things within me, things only half-done or done but eluding me, like the tying of my shoe laces, trying to soap my face with my one still-functioning hand, or squeezing out the toothpaste and having it land on the toothbrush. How demeaning, how degrading, always having to say thank you. And that surge of anger at every little mishap, an uncontrollable urge to break and to smash things. I pound the table, I pound the sink, I shut my eyes in the vain hope of it all vanishing and me being well again once I open them—how futile.

4

Was I always like this? I wonder. *Is this the real me, dormant until now, caged all these years, held in check only to become awakened by the ravages of the stroke?*

"Brain hemorrhage, brain ... left side, right side ... brain ... brain," they whispered at the bedside, and it reached my ears like echoes of far-off shouts, and I could perceive them long before I knew where I was and what really happened. The man looking down at me wore a white coat. So that was it. A hospital. And suddenly the room would plunge into darkness, and then the light would come on again as if some prankster was standing by the light switch, playfully turning it on and off.

And then came noises. Incessant and repetitive, some near my ear and others from far off. "Can you hear me, Nathan? Can you see me, Nathan? Sounds, manmade sounds, reverberating, bouncing off one wall and coming back at me until I had to shut my eyes and shake my head to make them go away. I wanted to say something, ask something, hear my own voice. I opened my mouth, I moved my lips, but there was only a grating, rasping sound and not my voice. I would suddenly become frightened with an overwhelming need to weep, and I would cry out, "Mameh," the only word I recognized as mine. The doctor, a young man, his was the first face I saw after I awoke. I wondered where I was and why my hands were tied down to the bedside railings. Prison bars, they seemed at first. A cage with chrome prison bars, the cage tilted, my legs higher than the rest of me, and I was afloat, unable to right myself, and I kept tugging at my wrists tethered to the bars.

It took days before I fully comprehended where I was and many more before I could recognize my son, Robert, and his wife, Margot. They told me that I kept saying no, no, no, and that I wept each time I looked at my inert left arm and nearly lifeless left leg.

"A matter of a couple of weeks," they said as they brought me here. They lied to me—my son and his prissy wife, the young doctor and the nurse, the whole lot of them. Two long months now—or is it three? I should have known they wouldn't tell me the truth. It was written on their faces. But then I so wanted to believe them.

I was not the model patient, not one resigned to having had a stroke. Nor would I meekly accept that asinine proposition of, "Thank God you're alive. So many never make it." I ranted. I raved at one half of me gone, or nearly gone, as if some cruel being had taken an ax, cleaved me in half, and left that useless part behind as a taunting reminder of the whole me I once was.

I'm still haunted by the memory of those frightful days and try to stave them off by reading the paper, writing a note, listening to my bedside radio, or simply staring at the polished top of my oak table and seeing all kind of faces in the pattern of the whorls—grotesque, some with elongated and droopy eyelids, some weeping, some grinning at me as if jeering.

CHAPTER
2

THE WINDOW, MY VISTA of the world. Dreary, this gazing at an autumn garden, at that one branch of a tree stretching across my window like a gnarled and withered arm slowly waving in the breeze. Or sitting and watching how the leaves ever-so-slowly turn yellow, then brown, then are torn off by a gust of wind and flutter away. I count how many are still left. And not far off from my window, a gray, old man sits on a bench reading a paper. When he gets tired, he simply raises his glasses toward his receding hairline, closes his eyes, and turns his face to the sky, trying to catch the few warm rays of sunshine, wane and feeble these past few weeks. He always wears the same short winter coat down to his knees, a mousy-looking fur collar raised to cover his ears. And there is his cane with a carved handle slung over the back of the bench. He sits there, hours at a time, immobile like a statue except for once in a while raising his head above the brim of his collar, blowing into his cupped hands, and pulling his head back like a frightened turtle withdrawing into its shell.

There was something familiar about the man when I first saw him. But these days, there are so many old men that look familiar. Age paints them in look-alike gray hues, wrinkles mar their faces, and flesh hangs limply from their jowls. But this morning, there is something new about the man. He pulls out of his pocket a folded newspaper and opens the pages with meticulous care, gently shaking them, then folds them over with a tap of his hand. He has done this before, but this time I can see the thickly printed headlines. German. From a distance, and with my eyesight far from what it used to be, I can vaguely decipher the word *Zeitung* ... something or other. The man reads. His head moves as he scans the lines, and then, as if trying to remember what he read, or perhaps his eyes have become tired as mine do, he closes them and raises his head to the sky where a thin sun emerges from behind the clouds.

And as I watch him, I wonder if he is asleep now or is simply brooding over something he just read, as I often do. Once again I'm struck by something familiar about the man's face, by his bushy eyebrows that come together at the bridge of his nose and are darkly contrasted against the grayness of his receding hairline, and by his habit of raising his eyebrows like a bird unfolding its wings before taking flight. He does that and throws his forehead into a series of washboard wrinkles. And I notice that the man has no neck to speak of; it's hard to tell though with that heavy coat and fur collar. After a while, the man goes back to reading and then neatly folds the paper before placing it into the side pocket of his overcoat. For a moment, he gazes in the direction of my window, his gaze somewhat unfocused but long enough for me to notice his deep-set eyes.

And that too is something familiar. The man has blue eyes, a watery kind of blue. Deep-set, blue eyes, thick eyebrows—I've seen the man before, a long time ago. My heart begins to race—a German. A heavily truncated man, broad shoulders, powerful arms, a neck so short that his head seems to grow right out of his collarbones, and the collar—always too tight around that thick neck of his. And the collar, yes, the collar, it used to be a uniform—a German uniform. I look at his face and try to recall where I saw him, the way one thumbs through a picture album in search of a photo pasted there a long time ago. I find it at last. My God, the ghetto! That's when it was. During the war. Nearly fifty years ago. A lifetime ago. The *Herr Arbeitsleiter*. He is there, and I see the man now. I capture him, yes, and with a pounding heart, I see him now, and along with him the time and its people I so want to forget.

My eyes are riveted on him, and the longer I look, the fewer my doubts. I can see him now. I see him as he walks with those long strides of his through the crowded ghetto sidewalks, expecting all near him to doff their hats and step aside. Dear God, I remember it now. It's all coming back to me, vivid and unmistaken. He's there, like a sleeping beast waking from its hibernation, stretching its limbs and yawning at me. It's there, and I haven't thought about it for some time. A forbidding vision it is, a vision that tags along the past, the unwanted past, the past I haven't thought about for some time. Ah, yes, his thick neck. He wore his German uniform then, tight fitting; it seemed to be strangling him, and he would raise his chin to free his neck from an encasing collar. And at times, in a foul mood, he would place his fingers between his collar and chin and twist his head from side to side. And those of us running into him and seeing him do that would scamper away, hide in the nearest doorway, step off the curb and into the street to look inconspicuous. A bad omen, this pulling his chin forward and loosening the collar. The *Herr Arbeitsleiter* was a man with a temper, and when in a foul mood, he would knit his brows, and his eyes would flash anger.

He was a man to fear. But in those days, all of them in those spiffy uniforms, their boots at high polish, riding britches, belt and revolver, were men to be afraid of. He never struck anyone, not that I ever saw. He would stop a man or a woman on the sidewalk, and using a swagger stick and without ever saying a word, he would simply point at the armband with the Jewish star that was all crumpled, way down the sleeve instead of in the right place above the elbow. He would then stand there and gaze at the man or woman fidgeting, trying to put it into place. Men would doff their caps, women lower their heads, and rarely would he acknowledge them with a short nod. But still we feared the man in charge of work. Too many would be snatched away, at times right off the street, and sent somewhere never to be heard from again.

Being near the window, I watched him with a renewed interest. Having given up his pursuit of sunshine, he shifts position and looks in the direction of my window once again. Long jowls, baggy eyelids, sparse hair, his hands tremble each time he turns the page of that newspaper, the pages fluttering like wings of a butterfly. I'm beset by doubts again—no, that couldn't be him. The man I knew, Gerhard Reichenberg, the Dog Catcher of the ghetto of Kostowa, we used to call him, he was young, in his twenties, perhaps early thirties, and powerfully built. He was young then, but then so was I, only seventeen and frightened. God, how frightened we were then.

The man rises slowly and with obvious effort. Holding on to the edge of the bench, as if afraid to fall back, he pivots around to reach for his cane and then stands on the gravel with his feet apart. The man limps, and shifting his weight to his cane, he drags the left leg, leaving a track of upturned gravel behind him. He proceeds slowly. No, that couldn't be Reichenberg, the man who would walk with a swaggering gait, his long arms swinging as if on parade, the people parting like water around the prow of a swiftly moving ship. He would walk as if he owned us, rarely looking at anyone, as if looking into our eyes was beneath his dignity.

Fifty years ago, it was. I vividly remember some of it. I try to remember more, but as yet I cannot. Like an aged rubber band, the memory stretches only so far and then threatens to snap. So much happened since then. And yet, that man—hard to forget the time when walking hurriedly, elbowing my way through the crowded sidewalk, I came around the corner, nearly colliding with him. We both halted, and the man stared at me angrily. My legs trembled. I watched him raise his swagger stick toward my head, I closed my eyes, convinced he was about to strike me, but the man tapped the visor of my cap with the end of the stick—I had forgotten to doff my cap. I did so hurriedly, and he walked on.

I watch him now as he walks down the path, dragging one leg behind him. He does it slowly, each step a visible effort. His eyes are riveted to his feet as if making sure he is placing them correctly—a stooped, old man, like so many of my friends and acquaintances these days. My kind of walking. Suppose I am mistaken. So many things are muddled since that damned stroke of mine—faces, names, dates, the whole world one large jumble.

The bench sits empty now. Wind-driven leaves flutter up and down like brown butterflies, some settling on the old man's bench and on the gravely path. I adjust the shades to mere slits. No sense staring at an empty, leaf-splattered bench and at an old man limping down a gravely path. Another image from the past, another visitation, this one in daytime. And there are so many, some of men and women I never saw, or think I never did. All bent on confounding reality, mixing the tenses, the past and the future walking in and out through that maddening, revolving door of my minds, of my mind.

Like the man on the corner where I lived before I had my stroke. The seller of papers in his makeshift shelter, bearded, his red nose forever dripping, and the man wiping it on the sleeve of his winter coat that he wore in all seasons. An identical twin brother of the beadle in our town of long ago. Each morning on my way to work, I would see him standing there, and like a wound-up toy, he would go through the same motions of bending down to pick up a paper from the pile near the curb, folding it into two, nodding his head at the passerby, most of them acquaintances of his, greeting them, handing them the paper, taking the money, reaching for the money belt, and clicking off the right change without having to count. One day, I walked over to him and tapped him on the shoulder. "Reb Mizrachi." I addressed him by the name of the beadle in my little town in Poland, and the man looked at me with the same cat-green eyes of the town beadle of forty years ago.

"An' the top o' the mornin' t' ye, Mr. Klein. And what

will it be this fine mornin'," he said as he handed me the same newspaper I had been buying for years.

Or the young woman at the grocery checkout counter with her arched brows, raven-black hair, a small gap between her upper front teeth. "Are you sure your name is Magdalena and not Malka?" I asked jestingly.

"Yes, sir." Magdalena shook her head. "But if you like, you can call me Malka. Better than Maggie or Marge," she replied with a pronounced Spanish inflection.

CHAPTER
3

I WAKE UP HAVING SLEPT poorly. Since that fatal day of waking up and realizing that one part of me took its leave, nights have become the realm of the illusory, of self-deception, of opening my eyes and wondering if I am awake or still dreaming. Kostowa, my hometown, was in the twilight dream of mine. It has been a long time since I dreamt of it. Small, dingy, crowded, a town no more than a hamlet, a fly speck on the map of Poland, a *shtetl* we used to call it. A dense forest like a black canopy covered the surrounding hills. A broad river skirted it, and a small brook ran through it, as if lost, trying to find its way to join the larger one. Surrounded by farmland, the hamlet spread along the flatland along the riverbanks. It was a place with no other reason to be where it was except the forest and the river to navigate the felled trees to the large saw mills ten kilometers down the stream, and then from there to the nearest railroad spur. A crumbling castle stood on a low hill, the seat of a former nobleman who ruled that part of the country.

I dreamt of Kostowa, another dream with endless variations, this one no longer of sunny days of being carefree and of light heart. This one was filled with anguish, the kind that blotted out all the days that preceded it. A dream of a single day that came suddenly like a scourge, darkness extinguishing every bit of light that ever shone there. A recurrent dream of uniformed men with skull and crossbones on their headbands on a rampage of killing. My dreams are silent like pantomimes, yet I wake up with a start, as I always do, and the vision vanishes.

Dawn creeps into my room, mere shafts of gray falling through the slightly separated slats in the shutters. I raise myself on my elbow. Down below, the garden and the empty bench are mere outlines. There is no old man there, and for a moment I wonder if there ever was one, or was he too part of that dream? The old insomniac that I am, I'm awake now, unable and not wanting to go back to sleep.

Miss Hedberg, my lavender-scented good-morning-wisher, barges in. The ride through the corridors gives her enough time to inform me of today's news tidbits—the love escapades of Elizabeth Taylor and some of the royal and not so royal families of Europe—or of the weather, which is perfect, the air crisp, the kind of air one can find only in Malmö, in her native Sweden, the wind-driven, cool sea air, good for the lungs and digestion, that is, if one sleeps with the window open, unlike most Americans who sleep in overheated and unventilated rooms. Miss Hedberg is a believer in herbs, fresh air, vitamin C, and prayer, though not necessarily in that order. A worshiper of the natural, she would go for a swim in the Baltic Sea in the middle of the winter, having to chop the ice away before she and a crowd of like-minded friends would plunge in. In the buff too, she claimed. Her prattle carries on through the entire morning exercises.

"Do you suppose we could try the walker again?" I ask, knowing full well that she will tilt her head and look at me with her raised, yellow eyebrows, as she always does when I want to do things she doesn't believe I am ready for.

"And the last time, if I hadn't been there just behind you, why, Mr. Klein, you could have fallen and injured that sore hip of yours. And what would I tell the doctor?"

"Please, just a few steps?"

"Ja, ja, Mr. Klein, but don't say I didn't warn you."

We walk inches only, her arm firmly around my waist, the rubber tips of the walker gripping the polished floor. I have to fight hard to keep my balance, but I'm upright and giddy with joy. I must look the way my little son, Robert, did when he first got up on his hind legs, let go of his mother's skirt, took his first step, and smiled at the world, his broadest smile yet.

"Not bad, Mr. Klein. In just a few days. Not bad at all," she assures me. "You keep it up, and with a little help, perhaps a brace around your knee, and we shall be ready for a nice little walk in the fresh air. Now one more step, a larger one, and don't be so afraid of leaning to your left side. You must trust yourself, Mr. Klein. You are all there."

And she lets go. I stand alone, grasping the chrome sidebars of the walker with all my strength. My heart races, and my head reels. With my feet riveted to the ground, I dare to lift my eyes, to let them roam freely. Silly, this moment of triumph—an old man standing in the middle of a room, looking at a large mirror and seeing himself stand, shoulders hunched forward, white knuckles gripping the walker bars. But why that haggard and grim face? I smile at myself, and the mirror smiles back, and so do the other mirrors, an infinite number of me, in front, in the back, and on both sides, an infinity of Nathan Kleins smiling back. Not much of a smile that, more like a grin, and I want to weep with joy, not grin this sheepishly.

I become distracted by the sound of soft clapping. Miss Hedberg stands there, right behind me and a little to the side, and smiles.

"And so you can smile, Mr. Klein. Ya, ya, and you can walk too. Now, if you promise not to try to use a walker unless I'm there to see you do it, I'll have one brought to your room this afternoon."

The walker, my new room companion, all shiny and inviting, stands near the window. I try it and nearly fall. If only I could cease veering to the left as if some invisible hand is pulling me over. And my left arm, better now, but still so feeble, and this hand of mine, how unwilling to grasp the side bar firmly. How many times have I gazed at it intently, willing it to move—a claw, a disobedient claw with merely a flicker of motion. Firm-fisted once, and yet nimble, my fingers were capable of deftly using miniature pliers to handle tiny wheels, spindles, and hair-thin springs to repair the smallest watches, and now they are so unwilling to do a simple chore.

During the early days of solitude, half-mad with despair, I would grasp my lifeless left hand with my right one and bring it to rest against my mouth to breathe against it. The breath of life, I recalled. *"And the Lord God ... breathed into his nostrils the breath of life, and man became a living soul."* Or that kindly prophet Elijah who *"stretched himself upon the child three times and cried unto the Lord ... and the dead child came back to life."* But to no avail, my unwilling hand weighing heavily against my lips remained numb. Or, while weeping over my helplessness, I would place my inert hand against my eyes, hoping to kindle life into it with my tears. And there were other times, times of anger, rebellion, of maddening despair, and I would keep hitting my hand or punch my disobedient arm, and when that failed, I would curse it, silently wishing my useless extremities to wither away, part from me, go and torment someone else. And I, the cynical nonbeliever, would remember the old Dybuk, that old folktale of an evil spirit that enters one's body by stealth to do its mischief there, and nothing but exorcism would expel it.

But then came a day when I cut myself. Trying to open a letter and using my left hand to weigh it down, my right hand slipped, and the sharp tip of my scissors went into the ball of my thumb. I felt it though, the pain surging up my arm. The wound bled. A few droplets emerged from beneath the cut, welled up, and ran down the side of my wrist in a tiny rivulet. I reached for some tissue paper, about to stop it, but at the sight of blood flowing from my wounded hand, useless and inert until then, I kept watching it with awe. My hand, my arm, they were alive after all, and my wounded hand seemed to be speaking to me. That useless appendage of mine, one I had cursed, upbraided, and renounced, was bleeding softly, and with that sanguinary message, it seemed to be telling me that it was part of me and as vulnerable as any other part. It seemed to be chiding me. I bandaged it with the greatest of care, and I wept. Tears of remorse and shame. A strange kind of reconciliation between me, Nathan Klein, and the left side of my body. But so many things were odd if not outright insane in those early days.

It is raining and gray outside. The days are getting shorter, and my eyes are growing tired reading. Another day, a day of no account. Once again, I indulge in the futile exercise of willing life into my hand. And at the end of the day, it finally comes. A spark of life. Like a small current, it runs through the tips of my fingers like the crawling of small ants. I raise my hand closer to my eyes in disbelief. It's there, the quickening of life, the kind my wife, Esther—may she rest in peace—once mentioned as she grasped the slight bulge in her abdomen, an angelic radiance breaking out in her face as she looked at me and said, "I can feel it, Nathan. So help me God, I can feel the baby."

I wait for a while to be sure that the flicker of life is not another one my delusions, but it's there. I let out a triumphant yell, and two attendants come running into my room.

"I did it! At last I did it," I keep screaming, half laughing, tears running down my face. "I tell you, I did it." I keep rubbing the tips of my fingers and squeezing them with all my might to make sure that whatever life has returned will not leave me again.

CHAPTER
4

THREE DAYS HAVE GONE by, and the old man on the bench is nowhere to be seen. I find myself repeatedly glancing at the window. The bench remains empty. It rained during the night, but now patches of blue appear in the sky, and sunshine floods the garden. As if freshly scrubbed and not yet dry, the wet gravel glistens, and so do the wet benches. A few patients—residents, they preferred to call them here—sit on some of the other benches along the path. His remains untouched, the fallen leaves plastered against the slats. The gardener, a stooped, old man with a grizzly beard, ambles by with his rickety four-wheel pushcart, the rakes, broom, and shovel sticking out like masts without sails. I watch him sweep a few leaves and meticulously deposit them into the cart. He does this with the reverence of a man in love with wilted leaves. He then puts the broom back into the cart and walks on a few steps. He does it leisurely and in slow motion, as if to underscore that gathering fallen leaves, new ones falling all the time, is a solemn ritual and must be done unhurriedly. He stops in front of the old man's empty bench, and using the broom, he sweeps some wilted leaves away.

Perhaps he knows what happened to the man. I open the window.

"Sir, please, sir!" I yell out, but the man pays no attention. I raise my voice, yet the man goes on with his sweeping. At last, having seen me wave my arms, he looks up, cupping his ear.

"That bench you just swept there." I point at it. "There is a man that comes and sits there every day. Do you know his name?"

He shakes his head and places his hands against his ear with a waving motion. I repeat my question, shouting this time at the top of my voice.

"The man, the one wearing a topcoat with a fur collar, do you …" I stop in midsentence as he continues to shake his head. He is deaf. I watch him go away, the pushcart wheels making a squeaky sound.

It's cold outside. From shouting through the open window, my breaths have become steamy. Too cold to keep it open. Perhaps too cold for the man to sit there on the bench sunning his face and reading that newspaper of his. Perhaps he moved, and I will never learn his true identity.

Miss Hedberg enters as she usually does at this time,

rosy-cheeked, her hair windblown. She trails a gust of cold air but is wearing only a flimsy, cotton blouse.

"Ja, ja, you men are all alike." She nods at the walker she had left near the window, now no longer in the same place. "And when something happens, who gets the blame?"

Feeling guilty like a schoolboy caught at a prank, I remain silent.

"Well, are we ready to use the walker all the way to our workout?"

We walk slowly, Miss Hedberg closely behind and to the side of me. We stop to rest for a while as she chats with some of the other residents, some on crutches, others in wheelchairs. We go through our daily paces.

The tone of her voice has changed. This morning, she seems less condescending. Seeing me make a fist, the tips of my fingers nearly reaching the ball of my hand, she tilts her head in admiration. "Now do it again, Mr. Klein," she says. "And keep on doing without thinking. Then reach for something and see if it happens again."

We walk back. I'm tired but exhilarated. Bound to a wheelchair only a few days ago, I now feel superior to all the others we pass. I chuckle, and for the first time in months, I hum to myself some self-composed ditty. The wheelchair, that love-hate object of mine, stands now in the corner, and I look at it with contempt. Even the room looks more inviting. My eyes are drawn to the window. He is there on the bench. His neck is wrapped in a shawl, the fringes sticking out above the fur collar. He wears woolen gloves, the thumb and index fingers bare, enough to open and turn pages. He is back to reading a newspaper, a folded section on the bench next to him.

"Ja, ja, another cold day." Miss Hedberg seems to have followed my gaze. "And old Gerhard down below is all bundled up for the winter."

She called him Gerhard. My heartbeat quickens. Gerhard Reichenberg. It's him, that crippled old man, bent with age, a cane next to him. Ah, yes, that cane, rubber tipped and shiny now—unlike the swagger stick of his with a small loop at the end. For a single flash, I see it pointed at my face, then at my forehead. It's all there as if it happened an hour ago—the stick, my cap, doffing it quickly. My hands begin to tremble as they did then. I feel a surge of hate for this man, a kind of hate mixed with fear I haven't felt for so long now, and I find myself gripping the handrails of the walker as if these were the handles of a deadly weapon.

"Miss Hedberg." I address her without taking my eyes away from the man. "His name, I mean his family name, would it be Reichenberg, by any chance?"

"Ja, ja, it's something like that, but we all call him Gerhard. I think he is German, a darling of a man. Do you know him?"

"Miss Hedberg, would you do me a great favor and take a note to that man?"

"You mean a letter? Why, Mr. Klein, he is right there. Just open the window and call out. If the two of you are old friends, what a surprise that would be … just … let me open it." She opens the window and cups her mouth with one hand, about to call out to him.

"No, no, Miss Hedberg, please." I stop her. "Here …" I take a sheet from the stack of writing paper on my desk, and using one of my crayons, I write down *"Kostowa"* in large letters, covering nearly one half of the sheet. "Just this, Miss Hedberg. Just show it to him, would you?" I hand it to her.

Slightly bewildered, she takes it from me and reads loudly, *"Kos-to-wa.* Just this? Just this one single word, Mr. Klein? Are you sure Gerhard here," she says with a nod at the man, "you're sure he'll know what it means?"

"He will. Oh yes, I'm quite sure he will, Miss Hedberg. Just show it to him, will you?"

She halts at the door, seemingly undecided. She looks at the cryptic message once again, frowns, shrugs, and goes, leaving me standing at the window, still clutching the arms of the walker. I can hear her footsteps fade down the corridor, then the opening of the door leading to the garden, and at last the crunching of the gravel as she walks over to where he sits. He either doesn't hear her approach, or if he does, pays no attention, engrossed it seems in what he is reading. She stops before him, and only now does he look up at her from above the rim of the paper. They speak, but with her back toward me, I cannot hear them. He nods his head though and moves his lips. She lifts the sheet of paper, and he takes it from her with one hand, the other still holding on to the newspaper.

My heart races as I watch this pantomime of the man taking it with his two denuded fingers, holding it before his eyes, scanning it back and forth, lowering it, then raising it again as if unable to comprehend what he just read. Then I see him stiffen and recoil against the back of the bench as if struck in the face by an invisible fist. He drops the newspaper and my note. Both fall to the ground while he raises his gloved hands and covers his eyes. For a long while, he sits like this, his head lolling from side to side as if saying no, no, that couldn't be.

All my doubts vanish. I see him now, Gerhard Reichenberg, the man of a long time ago. He understands the meaning of that single name of a town in Poland. A nothing town where all the Jews were murdered by his kind, and only I and two others survived. Ah yes, without a shred of doubt, it is the man, and he covers his eyes as if that single name blinded him like a flash of lightning. The *Herr Arbeitsleiter*. At the mention of Kostowa, I see him hurled back in time, his face contorted in a grimace of pain, the kind I felt just now writing that tragic name. I see it in the way he bends forward and buries his entire face in his dark woolen gloves. Glove-covered, his face looks like a black death mask.

Miss Hedberg must have realized what transpired and bends down to pick up the sheet of paper from the ground, reads it again, and shrugs. She reaches, touches the man's shoulder, and speaks to him while pointing in my direction. Gerhard takes his hands down, and his gaze follows her hand to where I stand at the open window. He leans forward, looking intently, and then, to see me better, he squints and shields his eyes with one hand. For one brief moment, our eyes meet. Half-turning, he reaches for his cane.

God, how I ache to lean out of this window and curse that man for all the years of pain his kind inflicted on me, for all the years of agony. Scream at him with every obscenity I have ever heard. Give vent to all that I have had to hold back for want of a face-to-face meeting with him and the likes of him. Instead, I mutely stand by the window, watching that wreck of a man, once the arbitrator of who was to stay in the ghetto to be left there, to go on living, and who was to be sent away to places one didn't even dare to whisper.

No, I refuse to speak to the man. Not now, not ever. I close the window with a loud bang and pull down the blinds. I lower myself into the chair, now fully aware of how badly I'm trembling. I look around me—the cot, the table, the wheelchair in the corner, the chrome walker near the window, the painting on the wall, the daily sameness of the room, the sameness of the buildings and the garden. Suddenly it all becomes unclean, polluted, filled with abhorrence.

Uneasy and jittery for the rest of the day, I barely touch my food. I call my son, Robert, just to hear a familiar voice. He speaks, and I pretend to listen to his prattle, his incessant complaining about his wife, Margot, the spendthrift, how she is becoming the spitting image of her mother, both in looks and mannerism, followed by his usual outpouring of excuses for not having visited last weekend. We have not been on the best of terms for a long time now, my son the perpetual complainer, the tire kicker, the fault finder with all except himself. After I lost my Esther, we drifted apart, the only thing still in common being the memories of some happier days, but even those are tarnished by this petulant and forever-complaining son of mine.

CHAPTER
5

It is late now. The afternoons are getting shorter with each passing day. Dusk drifts into the room, a twilight darkness, a gloominess mirroring the state of my mind. I keep staring at the window, and the naked branch silhouetted against the fading sky moves up and down in the wind like a conductor moving his baton. I try to capture some of my thoughts, hold on to them for a while, but all vanish as quickly as they come, like a landscape viewed from a fast-moving train. After a while, resigned, I let my thoughts become a single blur.

A soft knock on the door disrupts my state of dreamy oblivion, and I flick on the small table lamp.

"May I come in?" Miss Hedberg asks softly.

No barging in this time, she waits, and when she finally enters, I'm taken aback by her changed appearance. No white smock and no white tennis shoes, instead she wears a woolen knit dress, a single strand of amber beads, and matching earrings. Her high-heel shoes make her look taller and more slender. At first she stands near the door, apparently undecided whether to come nearer. She carries a leather handbag with a strap around the shoulder, clearly on her way into town for the evening. She hesitates before sitting down, placing the pocket book in her lap. Demure, almost retiring, she is a new Miss Hedberg, no longer the imperious physical therapist. She is young and pretty with lipstick accentuating her thin lips, her eye shadow adding color to her otherwise colorless face, and her hair done up in small curls around her ears.

Even her voice has changed from commanding to mellower as she starts after a moment of hesitating. "You must forgive this intrusion, Mr. Klein." She clears her throat. "But you see, this morning you sent me on an errand that turned out to be … well, how shall I say it … less than pleasant. In fact, more than that, a better word would be disagreeable. It has been on my mind all day long. Do you mind if we talk about it now?" She looks at her wristwatch. "Ja, ja, Mr. Klein, had I known what it was all about—and mind you, I'm still only guessing—I would not have lent myself to bring so much unhappiness to a sick man like Gerhard."

"I'm sorry, Miss Hedberg, but at the sight of this man, I couldn't think of anything else. I didn't intend to hurt your feelings."

"You see, Mr. Klein, the man wept. And I've known Gerhard for a long time, and he's not a weeper. Ja, ja, don't look so surprised. After you closed the window in his face, old Gerhard, that kind man, wept like a child. He wanted to walk over, reach way up, and knock on the window, and he nearly did so, but at the last moment, he turned around, wiped his eyes, and kept muttering to himself in part English with a lot of German words mixed in. 'He'd never understand,' he kept saying, '*Nein, nein,* no one would.' And there was one quite distinct phrase, '*Schulde, meine schulde.*' Sounded like guilty, or my guilt."

She clears her throat several times, and for a moment, I think she may break onto tears.

"And another thing, Mr. Klein," she says, "whatever it is that you wrote on that piece of paper, Gerhard is a sick man, and they tell me he has gone through an awful lot in his life."

"Ah yes, Miss Hedberg. Of course, he did." I try to speak calmly but am aware of sharp edges forming around my words. "Every one of those Germans went through, as you call it, 'a lot in his life.' War, occupation, air raids, their innocent Deutschland attacked from all sides. This one lost a brother on the *Ostfront*, that one lost a wife, their homes a pile of rubble. Poor bastards. Look what they had to endure trying to save the purity of their race, *Rassenreinheit*—racial purity, and all that crap, if you forgive me. I've heard it so many times. And now they feel sorry for themselves. Did you say he wept? Real tears, I bet."

My outburst over, we remain silent. I realize how my anger, clearly not directed at the woman facing me, touches her like an ill wind, and I can see how pained she is, the corners of her mouth drooping and her gaze directed at the pocketbook in her lap. She raises her eyes, intending to say something, and then slowly shakes her head from side to side, and our silence goes on.

"Here." She opens the pocketbook and reaches inside for an envelope. "I meant to give this to you tomorrow, but Mr. Klein, if you had seen Gerhard, I just couldn't wait."

I thank her and place the envelope on the table. She closes her pocketbook with a loud snap and stands up to leave. Near the door, she slows and, with her hand on the doorknob, turns once more to look at me.

"Two such fine gentlemen, you, Mr. Klein, and old Gerhard, and so much grief. Will there ever be an end to it, Mr. Klein?" She shakes her head as if wanting to continue but changes her mind and leaves, softly closing the door.

For a while, I listen to the high-heel steps fading in the distance. I'm alone again, staring at the letter right next to me. My first impulse is to tear it into tiny pieces, unopened and unread. A symbolic defiance of the man. My way of saying to him that there is nothing that he, *Herr Arbeitsleiter* of many years ago, and all his kin could possibly tell me that would undo what they have wrought. And without reading it, I'm denying him the opportunity to apologize, if that is what this letter intended. No forgiveness, *Herr Arbeitsleiter.*

I pick it up. How weighty and oppressive it feels to my touch. How offensive. The man who once pointed his swagger stick at my head like the muzzle of a gun wrote my name on the envelope, *Mr. Nathan Klein,* in his calligraphic and pompous lettering. Mr., he wrote. No longer, *Du Jude,* and there inside is a missive, to me, to the man he once so despised. And as I hold it, I become aware of my trembling hand grasping the letter. *Am I still afraid of him?* I wonder. *Am I still under the curse of that unspeakable fear these men used to arouse in their victims? Am I still possessed by that maddening terror brought on at the mere sight of the swastika, the sign of a double lightning bolt, of a skull and crossbones? No,* I decide, *I will open and read it.* Not to do so would be a tacit admission of still being afraid. And that I must not let happen. I will open and read whatever lachrymose message it may contain. Read it and then tear it to pieces. In front of him, if I can manage it, and throw the scraps in his face and watch him squirm.

Only two pages of faintly lined paper, the letters orderly, the words neatly spaced, some of the letters angular with traces of the old German Gothic script.

Tuesday, the 16th of October
Dear Mr. Klein,

This is surely the most difficult letter I have ever written. For a long time, I sat, pen in hand, not knowing how to start. Kostowa, that one word you wrote on that otherwise blank piece of paper was more eloquent than you realize. To say it was like a thunderbolt from a clear sky would hardly describe how I felt reading it. I pray to God that you will let me explain why.

Unfortunately, I know full well what happened even though I was not there at the very end. I was called back to headquarters, and when I came back to Kostowa, it was all over. I tried to find someone to tell me what happened, but to no avail. To my inquiries then and to those in the years after the war ended, only two replies arrived, both in the form of terse invectives. I had nearly given up hope when your note arrived. The pain and the anguish—it all came back.

Let me only tell you that Kostowa too was one of my life's greatest tragedies, but let me add that in no way am I trying to compare what happened to me with the tragic events that befell you. And for that matter, to all of the Jewish people who resided there. Nothing could ever be compared to that, and I pray to God that it never happens again.

Kostowa, that innocent, little town, became a turning point in my life. I know, this must sound trite you, my dear Mr. Klein, and you may find it hard to believe, but it was Kostowa that in large measure was responsible for me being here in America.

To be able to speak to you, after having given up hope to ever speak of it to anyone, would be more than I ever hoped for. Yesterday, *looking at that piece of paper, I had an urge to do so that I could hardly control. I wanted to rush across that patch of lawn and come to your window and plead with you to let me speak, but at the last moment, when I saw your anguished face and the way you shut the window, I realized that I had no right to do so. You had endured enough without having an old man like me bring it back.*

Should you choose to ignore this long missive of mine, (too long, I'm afraid,) I shall fully understand. Rest assured, Mr. Klein, that I shall not disturb you again. (I may even change benches to be out of your sight, if you so wish.)

Respectfully yours,
Gerhard Reichenberg

P.S. By any chance, are you in touch with any of the people who may have survived? G/R

The pages in my hand tremble, and I have to put them down on the table. He wrote in English. Somehow it doesn't fit the man. German was the only language I heard him speak. Of course it was in English; fifty years have gone by since I last heard the man speak, nearly a lifetime, and he too has abandoned his native language as I have mine. And yet, as I read his words, somewhere in that alchemy of my brain, each English word of his becomes transmuted into the German language. Dear Mr. Klein—*Mein Sehr Geehrter Herr Klein*. Respectfully yours—*Höflich Ihrer ...*

I read on. *"I pray to God ..."* The man, the insolent man of yesterday, calls upon God. A metamorphosis, another transmutation. *Herr Reichenberg*, whatever his rank was in that ungodly horde, has become a man beseeching God. Twice in his letter does he plead with that deity of his to be able to speak with the likes of me. And then he wants to know if there were others who survived. What hypocrisy. He too claims to have been a victim, though unlike so many of his fellow Germans, expresses no self-pity, does not present himself as a poor, innocent man caught up in a whirl of events, none of his own making, the way so many did. No groveling there, no entreaty for wrongs committed, a thing I found so repulsive in his countrymen after the war. Still that language of his, formal and stuffy, how correct each word. The same formal placard words, public announcement words, stultified and cold—*Achtung!* words, we used to call them. "On such and such a date, the following are to assemble in the square ..." Words I once read teary-eyed and with a chill running down my spine.

I put the letter down and stare at the two pages spread out on the table side by side, seeing only a blur before my eyes. It's dark outside now, and I'm tired. Too much exercise on the walker, too much turmoil that seems to have jarred me to the core. The past has come back for one more visitation at daytime, no longer a common nightmare. As a sudden gust it came, like a hurricane, a whirlwind from which I'm unable to extricate myself.

I open the drawer in search of pen and paper. Haven't written much lately. In the beginning, I wrote just to prove to myself that one side of me was hale and to all those well-wishers who, without saying so outright, looked at me with that stare of pity one reserves for a cripple. Cripple, like hell. And so I wrote, much of it sheer nonsense. In time, writing—just for the sake of writing—became a damned chore, and there really wasn't that much to write about.

Inside the drawer, the usual clutter of things. A stapler, paper clips, extra keys to my apartment, a stack of get-well cards still waiting for my reply, a bundle of plastic credit cards, my driver's license with the man in the mug shot looking straight at me with a sheepish smile, and for a brief moment I cease rummaging and stare at the picture. God how I aged since it was issued. Black and white, the flash renders the face ashen and flat like a mime with his face painted chalky white. Still, it is my face, the features symmetrical then, none of that crooked mouth of mine, one cheek flatter than the other, one eyelid drooping more than the other, and none of that hang-dog countenance.

A driver's license. My mind strays again, becomes sidetracked, and staggers off into the past, reeling like a drunkard. My car, obedient and forever patient, springing to life at a touch of mine. Such a long time now since I sat behind the wheel and listened to its soft purr. I bought it after Esther died ... ah yes, and before that, we had an old station wagon. But they made me sell it, trusty and comfortable as it was. A bit like me, that old station wagon, now that I think of it. Times of joy in that car and times of heartbreak. Esther was there in the front seat, an indispensable presence, as indispensable as she was in all other matters. Then came a day when she was no longer in the front, right next to me, close enough for our shoulders to touch. In the back, she was where she could stretch out her painful leg and put a pillow underneath it. How quietly she suffered those last few months as we drove back and forth to her radiation treatments, most of her bones riddled with cancer. I would look at her through the rearview mirror, the brim of her hat low over her forehead to conceal her near baldness following chemotherapy. She would look back and smile. A compound smile, full of apology for being ill and having to die. A good-bye smile of having to leave at a time when we, just the two of us, were free at last, no children to intrude into our well-being.

Then came the day when I drove her to the hospital, backseats down, a soft mattress and downy pillows under her head and her painful legs. I drove slowly to avoid ruts and bumps and looked more into the rearview mirror than at the road ahead of me. She didn't want an ambulance.

"That's how they take people to the hospital to die," she said, half-whispering.

I drove back from the hospital not daring to look into the empty mirror. For a long time thereafter, I still didn't, using only the side mirrors as often as possible.

I flip aside the pile of cards. The stationary is in an ornate box, pink sheets and matching pink envelopes—too intimate, too cozy, too affectionate for what I wish to say to that man whose writing lays on the table. I take another sheet, white, almost angry white like my thoughts, wondering if I should reply or simply ignore him. With my pen poised, I glance at his letter.

He addressed me as *Dear Mr. Klein*, and I wonder, should I address him as *Dear Mr. Reichenberg?* The word *dear* rankles. In my mind, *dear* and *Herr Arbeitsleiter Reichenberg* of years ago are mutually contradictory, one putting a lie to the other. *Herr Arbeitsleiter*. I write it on the margin of the newspaper and look at it. An insult, perhaps unwarranted now, an injury to the man who begged to be allowed to speak to me. A fellow cripple, after all, in this large fraternity of other crippled beings sleeping under the same roof.

Esther, Esther, if you were only here to help me, you with that wonderful ear that knew how to listen and to say things, the right things, at the right times.

Tuesday, the 16th of October
Mr. Reichenberg,

At the outset, let me tell you that having seen you from my window was like coming face to face with a nightmare. The kind I tried so hard to put behind me ever since that fatal day in Kostowa.

I have no idea if you saw what happened there. You said you weren't there when those thugs arrived to wipe out the entire ghetto, but to my mind, it doesn't matter. You were part of it, and I don't give a damn if you were the chief culprit or just an ordinary flunky. You were there with that swagger stick, that swastika armband, with that look in your eyes as if we, the people in the ghetto, were just so much garbage that needed to be discarded once and forever.

You wish to speak to me, Mr. Reichenberg? Please, spare me having to listen to your voice.

You seem to be interested in finding any survivors. I know of only three, including myself. The other two—I have no idea of their whereabouts. But there in Jerusalem, in a place called Yad Vashem, is a list of those who perished. If you are that anxious to come face to face with what happened, go there and look at what is depicted on those walls. If you dare, Mr. Reichenberg.

But please, don't talk to me about God. There were times when I was deeply religious—I no longer am—and to hear the word God uttered by your kind is an insult at its worse.

Nathan Klein

P.S. You need not change benches. An empty bench doesn't erase the fact that you and I sleep under the same roof.

I read the letter again. I'm not pleased. I should have used all the invectives I can think of, but there, hovering over my shoulder, is my Esther, invisible and inaudible to all but me, and she would have said, "No, Nathan. You mustn't stoop to their level," or something of that order. I let it stand.

How oppressively warm the room is now, and to make matters worse, the radiator begins its nightly clanking. I open the window just a crack, and a gust of fresh air rushes against my face and sets the pages on the table aflutter. It is still a chore to pick up things from the floor. The pages are strewn there, his and mine side by side, his in a neat, calligraphic script, the letters large, each capital letter with a small flourish, mine crooked as if written by an unruly schoolboy getting his homework done in a hurry. My eyes fall on the last sentence I wrote: *you and I sleep under the same roof.* A bit harsh. I scan his. *I pray to God that you would let me explain why.* I reach for the pen.

P.P.S. For the life of me, I cannot see the connection between Kostowa and you scurrying to America, unless you were guilty of something and had to run for your life.
N.K.

I place my letter in an envelope and stash Gerhard's away in the drawer with an uneasy feeling that this may not be the last I will hear from the man beseeching his maker to have a chance to talk to me.

CHAPTER
6

ANOTHER SUNDAY MORNING, THIS one wet but sunny, the rays reflected in myriad droplets along the naked branches. Wilting clumps of white and purple chrysanthemums, a spray of impatiens and primroses, the petals brown and drooping— vestiges of the summer that was. I never did like the transition between the colors of summer and the whiteness of freshly fallen snow sparkling like diamonds. Fall is the season of decay. Enough though. Too much as it is.

The bench is empty. Strange how that bench, one of many others, has assumed a new meaning. Even without that man sitting there, the bench has acquired a life of its own, a thing to draw my eye to, to call forth images of the present and of the past, interlaced with each other in a pattern as yet too intricate to satisfy my need for order. Time, that's what I need, time to sort things out in that crazy quilt of being thrown together with a man I once hated and feared, the same arrogant and haughty man who once held my destiny in his hand and now, enfeebled, that man is begging to speak to me.

I go back to my morning chores but soon become aware of crunching footsteps, someone walking along the pebble-strewn path outside my window. With my toothbrush in hand, I wheel myself to the window again. It isn't the man. A plump, matronly woman drags a little girl by the hand, the child walking reluctantly, one free hand clutching a small bouquet of pink flowers. A little boy walks tardily behind them, kicking the pebbles with each step. Sunday morning, visiting hours, mother and children dressed nearly alike, ruffles and ribbons, patent leather shoes—visiting hours. I nearly forgot. I look at them wistfully, especially at the two youngsters. Blond, fair skin, red cheeks pinched by the chilly wind. How I would like to touch that silky hair and fine skin.

My visitors will come later. No little children, only my son. Solemn, self-important, he will sit on the chair in mock pretense of rapt attention while casting a sidelong glance at his wristwatch. Margot, my daughter-in-law, will accompany him. She will arrive with her perpetual smile, a fashion-magazine smile of a young woman skimpily dressed in a miniature bikini, lounging in a hammock against the background of an azure sea. How fake those demure looks with the batting of her false eyelashes. Ignoring commas and periods, her sentences flow into each other like the waves in that azure sea as she goes on, "Oh Dad of all the people why did it have to happen to you and haven't you had enough trouble in your life and we want you to know that we think of you all the time and cannot wait till you get better and come and stay with us."

And so they come, and so they leave with the same predictable carbon-copy hello and good-bye. In parting, my son limply shakes hands with me, and his wife purses her lips and throws me a palm-glancing kiss.

A knock on the door again. Miss Hedberg opens it only a crack and peeks in before entering.

"Are you respectable, Mr. Klein?"

I bid her to come in and for a brief moment forget that today is Sunday when all must be at rest, including those flabby muscles of mine. She enters, dressed elegantly, wearing a white turtleneck sweater, a dark flannel skirt, a woolen jacket with a stand-up collar, and a fine gold chain with a small crucifix around her neck. She wears a Dutch cap, a little incongruous with those stiletto high-heeled shoes.

"May I sit down?" She nods at the chair. "I was on my way to church but ..." She hesitates for a moment and crosses her legs. "You see, Mr. Klein, there is something on my mind ... well, I've been thinking about it ever since that altercation between you and Gerhard out there." She nods at the window. Without intending, my eyes follow hers to the empty bench.

"I don't believe he's there now, Mr. Klein. He hasn't left the room. Didn't even show up for breakfast, the poor man." She recrosses her legs and stares down at the tips of her pointed shoes, seemingly at a loss to find the right words.

"You see, Mr. Klein," she says, still not looking at me, "whatever may have happened between him and you—I suppose it must have something to do with the past—please, please, Mr. Klein." She shakes her head, trying to forestall any interruption. "Try to remember, both of you are still my patients, and I cannot help looking at you as two elderly men, both sick—well, not sick really, let's say unwell—and holding grudges against one another for things that happened such a long time ago, long before I was even born. In fact, most of us working here weren't even born then. Well, it's hard to explain, it's just such a long time, and I don't want to see you two getting more hurt than you already are."

"Miss Hedberg, when you use the 'you,' what you really mean is poor, old Gerhard, that kindly man who once …"

I stop, taken aback by the way she suddenly raises her head and looks at me, her eyes narrowed and full of reproach. No tears in those watery, blue eyes but so much sadness.

"Mr. Klein." She stops and clears her throat repeatedly. "Mr. Klein, we are not children." Her voice changes and becomes soft and melodic. She tilts her head to one side in a manner of chastising a child. "We know what happened during that war,

Mr. Klein. Gerhard, a German, the right age to have served in the military during that terrible war, and you being a Jewish man, probably just a boy or a very young man, ja, ja, and only God knows what happened there to your kind, and—"

"Miss Hedberg." I raise my hand to stop her. "Let's leave God out of this. Whatever God knows is God's business. It's what that kind Gerhard of yours knows and, of course, what I know that still haunts me day and night. And Gerhard was part of what happened to my kind, as you called it. Sure, he's your patient, but to me, he is just a plain thug that ought to have been put on trial and strung up—remember the Nüremberg trials and all those bastards claiming they were innocent of the murder of so many—"

"You stop that, Mr. Klein!" She doesn't let me finish. Angrily, she uncrosses her legs, her back stiffens, and she forcefully grasps the armrests of the chair. "This place is a home for the sick, not Nüremberg, and he is not on trial here, Mr. Klein. Gerhard is just a sick man, and only God knows how little time he has left with the way things are going. If you must go on squabbling over who did what to whom and why, please, Mr. Klein, do so at home when you are all well," she says angrily through narrowed lips.

For a long while, we sit facing each other silently, me in my wheelchair, my right hand clasping the side arm, and she in her chair, her hands folded in her lap. We avoid looking at each other, our gazes directed at the partly shaded window. She is wrong, I feel. Dead wrong about the man and about how I should feel about him, here or anywhere else. And yet, against all logic, I feel chastised by this woman who, for so long now, would propel me each morning through those long corridors as if the wheelchair were no more than a stroller, and then bracing me like a child would try to ease me out of my chair and onto the exercise couch.

She is angry at me. I can see it clearly in the way she refuses to meet my gaze. I have no right to make angry this woman of infinite patience. *"No, Mr. Klein. Just lift your leg, Mr. Klein. We can do it, Mr. Klein. Ja, ja, there you are. Now that wasn't so bad, was it?"* I have no right to anger her, to enlist her as an ally in my loathing of that man.

"If you don't mind, Miss Hedberg." I hand her the letter I wrote. "I could mail it to him, but that would be silly, wouldn't it?"

She looks at me again, and this time a sad, forgiving smile breaks out on her thin lips. "Yes, Mr. Klein, that would be childish." She opens her purse and places the letter inside. "I'll be late for church." She looks at her watch and rises to leave. "The old pastor has a habit of sending you withering looks if you're late and he sees you coming down the aisle while he is in the middle of his sermon."

She leaves. A cold gust of air blows through the window,

and I close it. The sky is cloudy again, and a fine drizzle settles on the windowpanes, the droplets coalescing to become small rivulets. The trees outside the window, the garden below, and the bench turn into a streaky blur as if painted on a blotter. A day to read, to watch the football game, some of the finer points of that game still a mystery to me. Having witnessed so much mayhem in my life, this gratuitous violence still rankles. Eleven men on each side—all very wealthy by now, I was told—running and colliding with one another, hurting and causing pain and at times severe injuries, and all this while the crowds cheer wildly, and half-naked young girls kick up their legs and wave pompons.

Gladiators. Only the lions are missing.

CHAPTER
7

AT LAST, MY VISITORS arrive, breathless for having to walk all the way from the parking lot to my room. I sit and listen to what is going on in the outside world, including the sale at Gimbels and the recent acquisitions of paintings at the Museum of Modern Art, most of the artists' names unfamiliar to me. Some I have seen and remember only as ugly streaks and blotches of paint. Margot seems to swoon at the mere mention of such luminaries as Motherwell, Kline, De Kooning, Warhol, and other masters of the spray paint canisters and of blobs of paint hurled at a canvas. And I listen to the jabbering of my son, Robert, who finds the ultimate of beauty in the streamlined shapes of the latest Jaguar model, the intoxicating aroma of leather upholstery, and the purring of the motor like a kitten. He refers to his automobile as a she.

Smug, self-satisfied, a loud necktie, a checkered sports jacket with padded shoulders, the jacket and the pants way too large for him. I look at him and try to remember the boy who once delivered local newspapers and used the money to buy baseball cards. A fair student then. No, I never approved of his choice of a bride, his Margot, the only child of a wealthy wholesale furniture merchant from upstate New York, Margot the only heir to a fortune.

"Why should my Robert work?" she asked shortly after we met. "There is more than enough for the two of us to enjoy life. Now, why should he?"

And for once, I was at a loss for words, trying to explain to this young woman the hazards of idleness. Alluringly dressed, she would spend part of a day at the beauty parlor underneath a drying helmet, her eyes riveted to the pages of a fashion magazine, while Robert sat right across the mall having his nails done before they went off to their bridge game at the club.

A long way now since that little boy of mine would rush home from school to show me his little poem, a silver star appended at the bottom. I listen with feigned interest to what they say. To change the subject, I hand them a newspaper section. I do it with my left hand. I do it slowly and laboriously, raising my left shoulder. How hard I worked at that small gesture these last two weeks. A little triumph of mine, and they fail to notice it. By chance, it is the travel section of the Sunday edition, devoted to travel along the Rhine with its castles and vineyards, the front piece showing a photo of the rock and the statue of the Lorelei.

"Wouldn't that be wonderful, Nathan!" Margot exclaims, having mistaken my proffering of the section for an invitation to go there. She called me Dad throughout the wedding, and the day after changed it to calling me by my first name. It rankles me to no end. And so do the pictures of the River Rhine, the German castles, and all those picturesque marvels of their Deutschland. My son, apparently still dreaming of the beauty of a Jaguar, seems not to have noticed. They get up to leave with the promise to come back soon. Margot, lingering behind, continues about a new play on Broadway, "You must get well and see it, Nathan, it's a smash hit, and Edward playing the lead role, a real darling, the sexiest man I had ever seen, and if I were ten years younger I could fall in love with him and ..."

The door closes behind them, and my eyes wander to the streaky window. Visiting hours have come to an end, and footsteps recede down the corridor. Doors are being slammed. There is again loud stomping and a man's voice saying, "C'mon, Mary, it's gettin' dark, and Mama needs her rest." Then comes the revving of a motor and the honking of a horn in the distance. At last, quiet. The outside world of wellness has paid its dues to us, the residents here, and its members are now on their way home.

Home, wellness, men and women walking upright, some

running. I still cannot accept my state of being half-well—half-cripple, the half-well made prisoner by the lame. I move my arm, try to extend my leg at the knee, halfheartedly make a fist—I do this each time I reminisce about what it would be like to run again, swim, go for a long walk in the park, stop, bend down to inhale the fragrance of roses in bloom. I go through these repetitive motions the way another man would say his prayers.

It's time to read for a while, so I turn on the lights.

A white envelope peeks from under the door.

CHAPTER
8

I'T'S A LETTER, AND I wheel myself over to pick it up. No stamp.
My name is in that calligraphic script of his. He must have
brought it himself. Strange how my eyes keep returning to that
bench, and even now with dusk outside my window and a fine
drizzle casting an autumnal haze on the landscape, I expect him
to be there.

Sunday, the 19th of October
Dear Mr. Klein,

*I now realize how painful it must have been for you to come face
to face with me. At the risk of offending you again, allow me to add a
few notes about matters I should have mentioned in my last letter. It
was incomplete, but how does one compress events of so many years
into a single note written in a state of great agitation? It fails to tell*

you why I was so deeply moved at the sight of you, even though you closed the window at my approach. It may also explain why I persist in getting in touch with you.

You see, Mr. Klein, I so badly need to find some information that I had sought for so many years now, unsuccessfully, I must add.

Her name was Esther Stern, though she called herself Esta, a common variation of her first name. I have been searching for her since the day I returned from Cracow and found that Kostowa had been liquidated. There were no Jews left to tell me what terrible things transpired there during my absence. I tried to find out from the Poles living in that town, surely eyewitnesses to what happened in my absence, but they were evasive, probably afraid to even speak about it, especially to the likes of me. I walked through the empty ghetto—not a living soul. But the traces of what happened spoke more eloquently than words. It was the most chilling scene I had ever witnessed. Sorry to bring this up, Mr. Klein, but perhaps you knew her and could tell me anything of her whereabouts.

I realize full well that the chances of her having survived to this day are extremely small, but still, I feel compelled to try to find her. It has been nearly fifty years since I met Esta and our lives became entwined. She was nineteen years old then, and if alive, must now be in her sixties. But I feel that I must never give up trying. She may be an aged woman now, and yet I still see her as the dark-haired, slender Esta, the girl who one day rang my doorbell and introduced herself as the maid assigned to me by the Judenrat of Kostowa to do *my house chores. She was a frightened, young woman then, but all were frightened of us in those days. And as it turned out, with good reason that I need not elaborate.*

I do not wish to burden you with my personal tale of why I'm searching for her. It's a long and complicated story, and a tragic one. You were there at the time, as you so clearly informed me with that singular page, the name Kostowa written on it in bold letters. Without knowing your age, you too must have been a young man then, and I dare hope that you knew her.

I would be most grateful to you for any information about Esta, even the most trivial items.

Respectfully yours,
Gerhard Reichenberg

I read the letter once again, hoping to find a message in it other than that of a man in search for something that took place half a century ago. And whatever that something might have been, he is clearly agonizing over it to this day. My eyes scan the letter repeatedly—same formal tone, same pedantic lettering. I also suspect that the man was afraid that I would not reply at all. Whoever that Esta may have been, she must have meant a lot to Gerhard. She must have been very attractive. Perhaps very seductive, and that alone may have been that main reason for the ghetto elders assigning her to be Gerhard's housemaid. In those days there were so many attempts to assuage, to placate in order to save lives at a time when death and destruction were the order of the day.

But why? A German, a former official, a participant in that grand butchery of theirs, why would he be searching for a Jewish woman, an adolescent then, probably an old woman now, possibly no longer alive? It is something I have never encountered before. I am clearly stirred.

And who was this Esta? This young woman he describes as *the girl who one day rang my doorbell and introduced herself as the maid assigned to me by the Judenrat of Kostowa to do my house chores ... and our lives became entwined.* I turn off the light and stretch my limbs, tired these last few days of making an extra effort at getting my left side moving. I can vaguely remember one Esta, but that one had brown hair and was far from slender. A common name, there were many other Estas; some were called Esther, some Estka, and there were several Stellas. And who was that slender, dark-haired woman assigned to him by the Judenrat, those detestable men, Jewish elders, representatives of the ghetto, self-appointed, most of them, who allowed themselves to be recruited in the service of our tormentors, though so many had no idea of what they would be expected to do in the end? And what was the relationship between this once arrogant Herr *Arbeitsleiter* and the young woman? Was she his mistress? Was she one more young woman selling her body in the hope to save her young life at a time when the entire world seemed to have turned against us?

And what about that young woman, Esta? Did she go to him on her own accord? Was she perhaps coerced to go there under some threat and, having accepted her assignment, loathed the man and the duties she was expected to perform? Was she trying to save her own life by doing it, or were there others—parents, siblings, perhaps that of her own child? Those were the heartbreak times of trading. First one's possessions, and when these ran out, there was nothing else left but their souls and bodies.

At last, wakefulness gives way to dream with its recurring parade of images, some utterly strange, almost grotesque in their strangeness. And among them was one Esta, a vague image of a young woman walking down the crowded sidewalk of the ghetto, carrying in one hand a pail, a bright kerchief wrapped around her plaits twirled in a coil around the back of her head. But was her name really Esta, or was it Andzia? And Andzia's complexion was olive. Gypsy, we called her, and her large eyes flashed anger. In my dream, I follow her down the narrow sidewalk, and as she turns her head to look at me, she is an old woman grinning at me with toothless gums. I fight my way back to reality and wake up with a start.

The room is still dark. The clock with its luminous hands shows half past five. I throw on my robe and raise the shutters.

Still night, yet so many windows are already lit. The people residing in those rooms are silhouetted against the drawn shades like actors in a shadow play. It seems that those behind the drawn curtains sleep as poorly as I do. Is it in anticipation of the one long sleep soon to come?

There on my desk are two letters—strange tentacles reaching to me from that one man behind one of these windows, a man so different from all the others. Like a bridge, they are, spanning the now with the past, unbroken threads, gossamer-thin yet steel-hard, refusing to snap, invisible at times, and yet there it is, the *Herr Arbeitsleiter* in search of an old Jewish woman, her face by now time-worn and yet to him still a slender, beautiful, dark-eyed, young woman, a figment of his imagination as if she and all that transpired between them became frozen in time.

I let the shutters fall back into place. His two letters are still there on the table, the first and the one just arrived. The last letter seems less inflaming and at the same time more painful to read. I find it galling, his description of walking through the empty ghetto within days after it happened. He had no business there walking through those empty streets, peeking into the alleyways. An intrusion it was into the sanctity of so many dead, wantonly murdered by some of his kind. I found it less galling to have learned of the Poles going there and plundering the things left behind, pretending not to know what happened. In their eyes, these things belonged to anyone just for the taking. But the

Germans had no right to be there, not the Gerhards, Heinrichs, Liebknechts, and whatever names they called themselves. A sacrilege, their strutting down those miserable streets, probably going there to gloat over what their kind had done.

And he too referred to what happened there as a "liquidation," that damned linguistic sleight of hand of theirs for murdering entire communities—the old, the young, and the small children in their cribs and mothers' arms. To liquidate, to make liquid, to dissolve, to make nonexistent, to burn to ashes—spine-chilling words, and to this day, the mere mention of liquidation darkens the sky at midday. But he spoke of one Esta with a note that bordered on an obsession. An Esta who in all likelihood perished along with the many others—perished, disposed of in some anonymous mass grave, the traces camouflaged and hidden from prying eyes. His Esta, he must have loved her deeply to continue searching for her for nearly a lifetime, or so his short letter makes me believe.

How incongruous this Herr Gerhard Reichenberg, tapping his boot with his riding crop as he looked at the frightened people stepping aside to make room for him on the narrow sidewalk, yet at the same time in love with a young Jewish girl. A mockery, a lie, either invented now or a perversion of what really happened there. And yet, there rang a note of sincerity in the pleading of this old man for a scrap of information about her. Was it real or just a chance encounter, another wartime love story between the most unlikely of two young people? And he was young, so damned young then, hardly any resemblance to that old and stooped man walking with a shuffle along the pebble-strewn garden path.

CHAPTER

9

THE FIRST RAYS OF sunlight fall on the rooftops of the buildings like splashes of yellow paint on a muted canvas. The first employees are coming to work. I can hear the slamming of car doors, the screeching brakes of an arriving truck, the whining of an ambulance just coming to a halt near the side entrance. Miss Hedberg, that ferryman of mine dressed in white, propelling me down the corridors for my morning session, is there among them. And while the wheelchair squeaks, she will bring me up to the latest installment of today's news. She will then proceed to stroke and knead my flesh with her deft fingers. Miss Hedberg, the soother of my aches and restorer of my faith that all is not lost.

"Just a little longer, Mr. Klein, and we will have you back on those …" This time, she points at the parallel bars. Last week, it was a trampoline. Tomorrow, it may be her jogging.

Silently, I go on blessing her strong arms, her soothing voice, and now that bittersweet mission of hers of being the go-between for two old men, a carrier pigeon of strange messages between one still full of hate and the other who strangely clings to a past, the kind of past most of his kinsman are eager to put behind them.

Although she doesn't show it, I sense a new intimacy springing up between us, one that seems to transcend the usual relationship of therapist and one in need of mending. On the way back, passing one of the windows looking into the garden, our gazes fall on the bench. Still empty. I turn to look at her face. She too noticed it and silently shakes her head. Back in the room, she halts and looks at the two letters spread on the desk.

"Two letters?"

"The second arrived yesterday in the late afternoon." I nod at the door. "Someone shoved it silently under the door."

"And I suppose he didn't knock, right?"

"No, he didn't." I shake my head. "But what makes you think it was him and not a messenger?"

"Oh, it was him," she assures me. "And you will answer, ja?"

I nod my head yes.

"And you promise to be nice and civil about it, ja?"

"Civil, yes. That, Miss Hedberg, I can promise, but nice—I'm not so sure I'm ready to be nice, as you say. Not to a man who—"

She stops me by turning the wheelchair abruptly and with ill-concealed impatience puts her arm around my shoulder to help me out of it. She is clearly cross and leaves the room without her customary halting at the door to see if I'm comfortable. My ears are by now attuned to the smallest noise, and I listen and wait to hear the fading of her footsteps down the corridor, but there are none. The door opens again, and she pokes her head in.

"I will, Miss Hedberg, I will." I hasten to assure her. "And I'll be nice, very nice, as you call it." She smiles and closes the door again.

Monday, the 20th of October
Mr. Reichenberg,

I found your note where you left it—under the door. At least you could have knocked.

At the outset, let me tell you that I was prepared to ignore it, but as you can see, I had a change of mind. By some unfortunate turn, the two of us are not alone here. Aside from sharing one roof and other facilities, there is Miss Hedberg. A fine, young woman who in addition to massaging my limbs has taken upon herself to massage my conscience and be a peacemaker. And of all people, between you and me.

From all I can tell, she doesn't have the vaguest idea of what really happened in that godforsaken ghetto and thousands of others like it. But she doesn't seem to give a damn. To her, you and I are two sick, old men who have problems that are much bigger than who did what to whom half a century ago. She is young then, wasn't even born yet when those locusts of yours swarmed all over Europe. Two sick men, we are to her, men with sick limbs, and in her eyes, this reduces us to a kind of common denominator. She probably treats you the same way as she treats me. A loving but bossy kind of mother. A spoonful of chicken soup in one hand, and a paddle in the back to spank our behinds should we misbehave.

Tomorrow morning, she will barge in here, and on the way to my morning exercises, as she tells me the latest news, she'll suddenly stop and just look at me with those blue eyes of hers and say, "Well, Mr. Klein, any news you wish to tell me?" And of course, I'll know exactly what she has on her mind—have I written to you?

And so here I am. I read your two letters and remain baffled. A former officer in the service of that Führer of yours, looking for a Jewish woman? And for the past fifty years? A former Nazi—and I'm sure that's what you must have been—looking for one Esta. Esther Stern, you said. And the reason for looking for her has something to do with redemption. I'm not sure you used that word, but to me, the meaning is clear. Excuse me for being crass about something you seem to be feeling deeply, but my first thought was that you must be some sort of a crazy man. You must have been a madman in the first place to have joined up with those thugs. What sane human being could have wanted to be—I may as well tell you what we called you then—The Dog Catcher of Kostowa? And if you were half-sane then, you must have become deranged afterward.

But to the point. There were dozens of Esthers there. Dark-haired, some blonde—your Aryan type—some old, some young. In fact, after the war, I was married to one Esther, may her soul rest in peace—now don't start any of your speculations, my Esther lived all her life right here in the States. And there were other things in your letter that puzzled me. I tried to figure out how one Esther and the events that took place in Kostowa were responsible for you ending up leaving home and coming to America. Did you by any chance think that you might find your Esta here?

And by the way, what about that cane of yours? A war injury of some kind? Another one of those highly decorated war heroes? Right after the war, stranded in Germany while waiting for someone to kindly open the door for the likes of me, I saw a lot of young Germans with wooden legs. So help me, I never saw so many men walking on wooden legs with their chest puffed out, chin up; you'd have thought they were on a military parade. There was one who lived in the same building, no heat, food unfit for a dog, tatters, and once in a while, he'd forget himself, and when I wished him a guten morgen, he would shift the cane from his right hand to the left so he could give me the Heil Hitler salute. The first time he did it, I wanted to belt him, but how do you hit a cripple like that? After realizing what he had done, he mumbled some dumb apology and quickly wobbled away.

Enough of this scribbling.
Nathan Klein

CHAPTER
10

Miss Hedberg arrives late. Her greeting is subdued, her eyes are downcast, and she hardly looks at me. A gauze dressing taped across the right side of her forehead partly covers her temple. Seeing me staring at it, she speaks impatiently.

"Not now, Mr. Klein, please." She shakes her head, visibly upset. "I'll tell you later on. Now you just lean a little this way." She clasps my arm to help me into the chair.

"Could I try the walker?"

"Not this morning, please. We're already late. Some other time."

It's a silent journey this morning. I want to give her my letter, but her silence is forbidding. It's only now, while I'm stretched on the exercise couch, that she begins.

"I should have known better than to rush at Elizabeth without first giving her a chance to get used to me. Ah yes, you don't know who she is. Poor Elizabeth, she hasn't been out of bed for two weeks. There she was lying with her knees and arms flexed, and just as I pulled the cover back, she began screaming, 'Help, help!' and lashed out at me with her fingers bent like claws. Lucky she missed my eye. It was close though.

"Now turn on your back, Mr. Klein."

Overcome by a sense of guilt for what was done to Miss Hedberg by one of us, I turn obediently, perhaps more so today than usually.

"That old woman Elizabeth, what's wrong with her?"

"Dear God, it shouldn't happen to a dog. She is a young woman in her thirties, mother of two children. She was walking across the street, a shopping bag in one hand and waving at one of the children to follow her. She walked right in front of an oncoming car. Was in a coma for a while, and now she's frightened, withdrawn, has to be fed and washed. The other day, I saw her husband and the two little girls—couldn't have been more than five and eight years old—doesn't even recognize her own children—her nurse tells me. Beautiful children. I felt like taking them in my arms and hugging them."

Her voice breaks, and tears well up in her eyes. "Mr. Klein, why does this have to happen to the nicest people in the world?" She blows her nose and dabs her eyes, then covers my legs with a bed sheet and proceeds with flexing and extending my arms. "Now, Mr. Klein, show me what you can do all by yourself."

I flex my arm, surprised at how well I'm doing it. "There, Miss Hedberg. I hereby challenge you to an arm-wrestling match."

"Oh, Mr. Klein, it's patients like you that make it worthwhile ... and Gerhard too," she adds. "Most of the people here are so ... well, let me say infirm."

"Decrepit, you mean."

"That is not a nice word, Mr. Klein. We mustn't use such words here."

Getting back into the chair, I hand her my letter for Reichenberg.

"So you did reply, Mr. Klein." She folds the envelope and places it in her pocket. Still sniffling, she smiles back at me, her first smile this morning. "But I knew you would reply. And just this morning I stopped by Gerhard's room, poked my head in, and said, 'He'll answer. You'll see.'"

"I haven't seen him out there the last few days." I nod at the window we are passing. "Too cold for him, or what?"

"Bed rest, the doctor said. Bed rest with his leg slightly elevated and in a tent."

"Did you say a tent?"

"Sure, a small tent stretched right over the leg so that nothing will touch the skin and to keep it warm."

He is ill. For days, the bench remains empty. Each time I approach the window, my gaze falls on it. Never thought a cheap, wooden bench could look so forlorn, the paint peeling, wilted leaves adhering to the slats, a few bird droppings in between. It is his bench now, and by a strange twist of fate, mine too. Each time I hear footsteps in the corridor, my eyes inadvertently wander to the door in anticipation of another letter. Three days after my note to him, Miss Hedberg brings one and hands it to me with a dimpled grin.

"How is he in that tent of his?" I ask, trying to sound as casual as possible, though for the last few days I kept restraining myself from asking.

"Still in bed and resting his leg. It feels warmer now. Ah, that Gerhard, he is a tough, old man. Those old Germans—hardy people, some of them."

"I bet they are, especially when it comes to—"

"Oops." She stops with my leg raised halfway in the air. "That was the wrong thing to say. Sorry about that, Mr. Klein."

As if sensing my impatience to get back to my room to read the letter, she hurries through the paces.

Thursday, the 24th of October
Dear Mr. Klein,

Thank you for your note. Miss Hedberg is an angel of mercy. I dare suspect that had it not been for her intervention, I would have been sadly deprived of your last note.

Forgive the somewhat scribbled writing, but sitting in bed is an awkward place to write a letter, especially if the one and only leg I still have is elevated. Allow me to reply to some of the questions you have raised. First of all, my cane and my limping. No, I've not lost my leg in the war. I did not receive any medals for bravery, as you intimated. In fact, I was never sent to the front. I have lost my leg in a much more prosaic way. And I pray to God that I may keep the one I still have.

You see, I have diabetes, Zuckerkrankheit they call it in German. I've had it since I was a youngster. That and having to wear glasses with special thick lenses made me exempt from serving in the ranks, as the say. A German soldier with insulin and syringes in his backpack and glasses with thick lenses was not exactly the model of Aryan masculinity. And so they assigned me to other duties. Thinking back with that proverbial wisdom of hindsight on what happened, I often wished they had sent me to the front. But here I go again, bringing up the past, the part that must be painful to you.

But how could I avoid it? It's the past that keeps the two of us apart. There is your window, Mr. Klein. I can see it from my bench. I can even catch the sight of it whenever I open my window and lean far out. And yet there seems to be a gigantic wall that separates the two of us, one I'm trying to breach. And judging from the tone of your letter, I'm not very successful.

As to Esta, I wish I could pour my heart out to you on these pages, but I'm afraid you may find it too long and tedious. Let me only say Esta was a woman I loved deeply. It may sound romantic, even trite, something out of a trashy novel. Kitsch-trashy, we used to call it. But you see, Esta was my first love, and with her gone, all else pales in comparison. And I still cling to the hope that she may be alive, perhaps under an assumed name. Perhaps she survived and went to Israel where she changed her name the way so many did. Many years ago, I went there to look for her. I kept wandering through the streets of Jerusalem, and then for a few more days in Tel Aviv. Sitting at one of the numerous sidewalk cafés looking at every dark-haired, slender woman passing by, I would completely forget that so many years later she may no longer look like that.

In your first note, you suggested that I go to Jerusalem and to the Yad Vashem. I did, Mr. Klein. But of that some other time.

They tell me that my leg is getting better and if all goes well I may be out of bed to take a few steps. In the meantime, I look forward to hearing from you.

Respectfully yours,
Gerhard Reichenberg

CHAPTER
11

Autumn days, vapid days, carbon-copy days of each other, days limping along as I do, the way my new correspondent does, days are suddenly disrupted by a storm. Daybreak is ushered in by a howling wind, and the sky, usually gray at this hour, is leaden. The wind-whipped naked branch outside my window keeps lashing the pane with a fury, and I keep staring at it afraid it may break the glass. Angrily, the wind, now a gale, sweeps the ground and raises the fallen leaves in a maddening swirl. I'm startled by the lightning, followed immediately by a crashing thunder. I always am. Somewhere down the hall, doors are being slammed. Irresolute footsteps pass my door and vanish, and a few shouts are soon drowned out by the sound of heavy raindrops pelting the window.

Miss Hedberg arrives, bouncier than ever, clearly invigorated by the storm, her reddened cheeks outright fiery this morning.

"Ja, ja, we have gales like this in Malmö." She nods at the

window and the rain coming down the eaves like a single sheet of water. "They come from the sea, suddenly. But it happens in spring, not in autumn, and the rains are heavy, and we run out into the rain, and we prance around and ..."

"In the nude, Miss Hedberg, right?"

"Ja, ja." She raises her head to the ceiling as if that nice, warm Malmö rain is about to come down, and she smiles. "But how did you know that?"

"Just a guess, Miss Hedberg. I still remember you telling me how you go swimming in the buff in the middle of the winter, chopping the ice in the ocean. Swedish women and all that. For a long time, I tried to picture you ..."

"Now, now, Mr. Klein, to speak like this is most unbecoming a refined gentleman like you." She tilts her head in mock reproach but blushes crimson just the same.

Its fury spent, the rain turns into a steady downpour, the only sound now, the soft drumroll of the raindrops against the window. As good a time to write as any.

Monday, the 29th of October
Mr. Reichenberg,

With each letter, you're getting to be more and more of an enigma. A Nazi at the Yad Vashem. This has to be a first. This is even better than a Nazi falling in love, head over heels, as you say, with some Jewish girl, then spending the rest of his life looking for her. According to Miss Hedberg, our letter carrier and peacemaker—she must have read somewhere that the peacemakers, or is it the meek, will inherit the earth—you are a kind man. I would like to believe that. I can feel the eternal optimist in me stirring. Optimism is a Jewish trait, you know. It's also the only thing left to the destitute if they wish to go on with their daily lives. Remember, we got our Messiah, that ultimate badge of the optimist. Righteousness, justice, mercy, and compassion, the kingdom of God to come at some indefinite time, and all that. Of course, you Christians had to go and do us one better by claiming that he had arrived and making him the centerpiece of your faith.

Sorry to be blasphemous.

When it comes to altering my image of a Nazi, something tells me that you have lots more up your sleeve. And while you are bedridden, and I in front of a window watching the rain-soaked landscape, you may as well let me have the rest of it. Paper, they say, is very patient.

And while you're lying there in bed, writing to me, one leg of yours gone, the other hovering between the realm of the living and the dead, good manners require that I wish you a speedy recovery.

Nathan Klein

His letter arrives a few days later. Something is happening to the man. I can tell even before opening the envelope. My name, usually written in a fine calligraphic style, betrays clumsiness, the letter K lacking the ornate wiggles, the other letters uneven, and the line slumped near the end.

Wednesday, the 30th of November
Dear Mr. Klein,

Thank you for your wishes for a speedy recovery. I would gladly settle for just a recovery, speedy or not. What ails me is the slow but gradual narrowing of my arteries. They say it's somehow related to diabetes. But now there is also pain. A toothache kind of pain in my whole leg, and it just doesn't want to let up. I shy away from taking drugs but finally relented in order to get a little rest. I feel doped, a thing you can clearly see in my clumsy penmanship. Unfortunately, it's only the lesser side effect of whatever medicine they give me. It's the thinking along with the writing that seems to be defective. I used to be good at it, my pen springing to life as soon as it was poised over an empty sheet of paper like a thirsty cat over a bowl of milk. I now have to force myself to form a single sentence, forgetting what I wanted to say before the sentence is half finished. Slow plodding this brain of mine. Reminds me of those overworked farm horses pulling a plow, and the peasant having to whip them.

Slow going, very slow. But I wish to reply. It's now very important to me. Don't ask me why, Mr. Klein. I wouldn't know the answer. All that I do know is lying here in the semidarkness, hour after hour, half-dazed yet unable to fall asleep, composing words, a sentence, then forgetting most of it by the time that I finished.

There is so much to tell, and I don't quite know where to begin.

Allow me to start with Esta. You must be wondering why of all things, an old man like me keeps coming back to what you alluded to as some kind of a love affair with a Jewish girl while she was nineteen and I was twenty-six, an affair that lasted only seven months and ended so tragically.

I'm sorry to have to go back to the past that you are so anxious to put behind you. But aren't we both the products of it?

As a diabetic, exempt from active duty on the front, I was assigned to be the Arbeitsleiter in your town. I must be frank with you and admit that at the time I was quite elated over the assignment. It was the late summer of 1943, two years since the attack against the Russians, when my orders came through. By then, that bright prospect of winning that vaunted Blitzkrieg and everybody going home to bask in the glory of another victory had turned into a nightmare, one more bubble that burst. Instead of victory, more and more letters were arriving every day to inform of those who had died for the glory of the Vaterland and the Führer. Those at home, the old, the very young, the women tending their homes, no longer walked with their heads high as if the world was just another plum ready for the plucking. To be exempt from military service was no longer a thing to be ashamed of, though no one dared to speak of it openly.

I arrived in your town, and this was my first face-to-face contact with Jews other than those who once used to be my neighbors, school mates, and fellow apprentices in my workshop. By the time I had gotten there, the Jews, as portrayed by the likes of Herr Goebbels with his Reichspropanda, *Herr Streicher and his* Stürmer Zeitung, *and others of a similar bent, had already bitten into my soul. I had finally come to believe that the Jew indeed was a despicable human being, a denizen of the sewers of the human race, the embodiment of all that was low and contemptible. Strange how I failed to connect the images of my former classmates, the people living in the apartment below us, with those caricatures staring at me from every scrap of newspaper and propaganda poster.*

On arrival to Kostowa, I was greeted by men appointed by the German authorities to police themselves. No need to belabor who these men were and what tragic role they were compelled to play, especially in the end. They cowered, cringed the moment I raised my voice ever so slightly. Men old enough to be my parents groveled before me, lowered their eyes, ready to bribe, to appease my slightest whim. Never in my life had I felt so important.

Heady stuff, Mr. Klein. Heady stuff to a young man of twenty-six, a member of the Nazi party, a believer that the Germans were truly the Herrenrasse, *the superior essence of humanity. Especially for a young man that until then secretly thought of himself as somewhat defective. My father, of course, made his contribution to it, and my comrades marching off to do their duty for the cause did their share. Here I was, intoxicated with my omnipotence. In the beginning, just walking through the ghetto, seeing all scurrying away, doffing their hats, bowing and scraping, as they say—how thrilling. And how venomous to the soul of a young man.*

I can imagine how offensive this must sound to you, Mr. Klein, and painful. But for once I wish to be as honest as I possibly can. I

was a Nazi. The real McCoy, as they would say here in America.
And no excuses here. I believed with all my heart in what it preached.
To me, and to my compatriots at the time, it was more than simply a
political credo. It was a new faith with all the trapping of a religion.
There was the ritual, the emblem, the new dress, the new haircut, the
new greeting, and above all the new God. A living God that didn't
reside somewhere in antiquity, speaking to you through some burning
bush on a mountaintop, or one hanging from a cross with a crown
of thorns and blood running down the side of his face. This one was
real, alive, powerful beyond imagination. A God before whom all
mankind quaked in fear. And you could see him standing there at a
rally, and you could hear his voice thundering down at you, and if
you ever doubted in what that new God said, all you had to do was
shift your gaze and look into the trance-like adoring eyes of the fellow
standing next to you with his arm stretched just as high as your own
arm. The Nazi salute. It was more than just another way of saying
a good day to you. It was the reaching out to that new deity.

Enough of those foolhardy days. You were there, and you must
have seen it, at least part of it. And to you it must have appeared as
the height of madness.

My quarters were near the entrance to the ghetto. Day by day,
watching the people leave to go to work for some war enterprise,
then coming back at day's end, tired and with shuffling gait, cowed
but still dignified, perceptions began to change. Subtle at first. The
elderly Jewish man who one day came to deliver an ornately carved

bookcase—one of those many bribes—looked at the piano in the corner—that too was a bribe—that hadn't been opened for God knows how long and asked me if I would like to have it tuned. I deigned to nod my head, and he came back the next day with his tools. After a while, he forgot the tuning part and played. The man was in a trance. I looked at his haggard face, his threadbare coat, frayed pants, scuffed shoes, and at his hands that moved over the ivory with agility I had never seen before. I sat down and listened, and the moment he wanted to stop, I shook my head and asked him to continue. He was a concert pianist who had performed in some of the finest halls in Europe and having been evicted from Germany came to the ghetto to live with his sister. Another man assigned to work in the garden, by then a heap of rubbish, was an attorney from Cracow. A man bent with age, a former professor of mathematics, was assigned to shine my boots and help in the kitchen. One by one, as I looked at them, ordinary men, craftsmen, intellectuals, those poster caricatures began to crumble; in their stead I saw men I had never seen before. The sly, villainous poster faces became faces of anguished human beings. And so many spoke the German language. Mine, warped by a strong local vernacular, paled in comparison.

Then one day she came.

She too was a bribe, I learned later. One of the many bribes that were wasted on me in the belief that I had anything to say in what eventually befell them. I made no attempt to tell them so and accepted their largess not so much for the intrinsic value of their *bribes as for what it did for my already inflated self. I was gone for a few days. On my return, I found her busy house cleaning. I was so used to being served, having my boots polished, uniform pressed, meals prepared, that I hardly noticed her at first; she was only one of the many in that entourage catering to my self-indulgence.*

It happened almost suddenly when she ceased being a faceless young Jewish servant and became a woman. Although it happened such a long time ago, I relived that moment so many times that I still remember it vividly as if it were only yesterday. It was the end of the day and time for her to leave. Before reaching the door, she untied her scarf and allowed her hair to fall over her shoulders. I shall never forget that gesture of her shaking her head to let her silken, black hair fall down evenly. She did it unselfconsciously, her slender hand reaching the nape of her neck and letting her hair cascade down. At that moment, our eyes met. I never noticed them before; perhaps I never looked at her until then. They were the largest eyes, deep brown and almond shaped, and I stood there riveted, unable to avert my gaze. She looked back at me as if she had been gazing at a mirror or at an empty space beyond where I stood, and there was neither fear nor boldness, and she left.

Strange how that one single glance, without the exchange of a single word, made me approach the window and watch her step to the sidewalk until I lost sight of her in the crowd of pedestrians. From then on, I sought every opportunity to be in my quarters just to catch a glimpse of her, the way she moved, the way she held a polishing cloth, the way she wiped the side of her chin with the back of her hand. Mesmerized would be a good word. It became an obsession just to see her, watch her move, listen to her humming to herself, unaware that I was within earshot. We rarely spoke more than a few words: her name, how old she was, and where she had come from. Her answers were curt, without a hint of fear and with an economy of words.

Her name was Esther, Esta to her friends. Her parents were someplace in Cracow, and she had no idea where they were. I so wanted to know more about her, but there was that look, a forbidding look in her large, unblinking eyes that kept you at arm's length from becoming too personal. It was only later that I began to read the finer nuances of her gaze. There was rarely surprise at anything that I said or the way I said it, as if she had experienced it all again and again in her young life. There was nothing new, nothing so enjoyable, nothing so terrible that she hadn't seen before, her eyes seemed to say.

PS. Sorry to have to stop here, but someone is at the door, and it looks as if the doctor and one of the nurses are about to pay me a visit. Will continue.

Respectfully,
Gerhard Reichenberg

CHAPTER
12

Miss Hedberg has gotten into the habit of carrying Gerhard's letters in the side pocket of her white uniform the way a postman carries them in his leather bag slung over his shoulder. He used personal stationary with an ornate border, and I can see the letter sticking out from her pocket the moment she opens the door. When she comes closer to help me into the chair, I simply reach for it and place it on my bedside table. And like that postman at home, she too grins broadly whenever there is a letter, and she shrugs when there is none.

Thursday, the 1st of December
Dear Mr. Klein,

Sorry for the delay. Doctors have a most unsettling habit of entering the room and speaking to the nurse without looking at me, as if I weren't present there at all. Having squeezed my leg, he felt for every inch of my artery—femoral, they call it—from the groin all the way down to my toes, frowning, closing his eyes in what looked like intense concentration, then raised my leg way up, then let it slowly down while watching it, mumbling something, the words sounding like tibialis, dorsalis, poplit ... something, while the nurse made quick, jabbing notes in the chart and mumbled with that ever-patronizing, "We're doing just fine, Mr. Reichenberg," and having finished with the ordeal, they left me more mystified than ever.

But now to go back to my lengthy tale about Esta (way too lengthy, I'm afraid).

One day it finally happened. That too is one of those moments deeply etched in my mind. She was about to leave, and by then I had made it a habit of following her to the door. She took off her handkerchief, and we nodded our usual good-bye. She stopped at the door, and without exchanging a single word, she began to unbutton her blouse. She must have known by then how much I desired her. Leaning against the door, she crossed her arms over her chest covering her small breast. Lowering her head, she ceased looking at me. I wondered if it was a gesture of shyness or perhaps one of resignation of someone facing the inevitable. Was she dreading what was about to take place, or was she bravely fulfilling a command given her by one of the elders of the ghetto in the hope of averting a pending catastrophe, similar to the one already taking place in so many other ghettos all around them?

She submitted with only a barely audible gasp. I was clearly her first.

I'm an old man now, dear Nathan, and I am still hounded by that image of a young maiden standing with her arms crossed, shielding her breasts, standing and waiting so utterly resigned. Looking back at that moment has been my self-flagellation all the years ever since that happened. I was young then, impetuous and heedless. Perhaps I still am. God, how I wish I could undo that moment. Undo it, and instead of acting so hot-headed as I was at the time, go over to Esta to embrace her, to caress her lovingly. But then aren't there so many "If I could only have ..." Our lives, my life is so full of it.

She submitted passively, as if this too was part of her duty, part of the finishing touches at day's end, like the folding of the blanket and turning back the bed covers for the night. Never a sound, just total submission, not even a pretense of expressing pleasure. Gently disengaging herself, she would leave seemingly neither disturbed by what just transpired nor pleased.

Only once did she veer from her habit of silently submitting. I could sense the slightest hint of passion, and only once did she utter a small cry. It could have been pleasure, but it could have been pain. I looked at her, and her eyes, those wide, large eyes of hers that never ceased looking at me, they welled up with tears. Sobbing, she dressed and as usual left silently. I find it difficult to describe those late afternoons only to say that the more she remained unresponsive, the more I wanted her, not only physically but also to give her pleasure, to see her smile. Of no avail.

On my part, it gradually became an all-consuming passion. One that erased all that I had ever been taught by the mentors of the Reich. It made everything irrelevant. I went to bed thinking of her and rose in the morning wishing she were there at my side. I looked impatiently at the clock, waiting for her arrival. At times it seemed like an obsession, like a madness. Call it by whatever name you wish—unrequited love, a wounded male ego, self-reproach for taking advantage of a young woman who clearly was there because she was ordered to do so, part of that never-ceasing bribing, or that look of utter vulnerability of hers, even while I tried to be as gentle as possible during those afternoons of our lovemaking.

Shortly before that ultimate catastrophe, she became pregnant. I noticed it, and she didn't deny it. Rudely, I asked her if I was the father or could it have been someone else, and she only shook her head. There was no other. I was the father of a child that would be born in perhaps three months. A Jewish child fathered by a German officer. The year was 1943.

Rumors of atrocities committed by our people against the Jews in the conquered cities and towns on the eastern front were rife. Some of my colleagues bragged about it quite openly. And there was hardly a day when new orders to tighten security around ghettos, to create rosters of men and women capable of working for the war *effort*—Kriegsnotwendigkeit—*war needs, they called it*—*their skills and all sort of irrelevant data were being prepared.*

I grew uneasy. Soon I grew frightened. For Esta, for the child, for those outside there in the street below my window, and for myself. I remember the first time after learning of Esta's being with child, I stepped out for my usual obligatory walk through the ghetto. Dear God, Esta's child, my child was one of them. And I found myself walking more slowly, gazing at the people around me. My child was one of them, and by proxy, I too was one of them. At the realization of it, I had to stop, lean against the wall, and wipe my brow. I was perspiring profusely. I felt like I was choking in that tight collar of my uniform. I went back to my quarters and spent the rest of the day pacing up and down, approaching the window, gazing down at the many hurrying by, wanting to open the window and shout. But what would I shout? That I, Gerhard Reichenberg, was in love with one of them and now the father of a child, my child, their child?

I knew all too well the consequences of such disclosure. The racial laws. How well I knew those laws of conduct of any German toward Jews in general and Jewish women in particular, especially as they pertained to a German, a member of the party wearing the uniform of the Reich. They had been hammered into me until I could recite them by heart like some cruel pater nostrum. All three of us would die, Esta first, along with the unborn child, and I next.

And there was no one to ask what to do, no one to share the anguish, not even Esta. The implication of what may happen if the truth was ever revealed was too horrid to even confide in her, to the woman I loved now more tenderly than ever. My medical checkup long overdue, I left for the headquarters in Cracow, to that seat of power over what once was Poland, to that beehive of activity where I was sure to run across an acquaintance, one I knew well enough to ask for advice without fear of betrayal. But all I encountered were long and stony faces. The news on the Ostfront was getting more devastating with each successive rainfall, and the onset of another icy cold winter that decimated the men the year before had already begun. I stayed for a week or so and headed back.

No need to tell you what I encountered on my return. The things I have written must be painful enough for you to read. Perhaps some other time. Let me just add: there was no one left to tell me if she was sent away, killed on the spot, or, as I so often cherished the fantasy, managed to escape that butchery, and she and my child were alive somewhere.

I should have been there when it happened, Mr. Klein. I shouldn't have left even for a day. Being there, I could have helped, I naively believed. And if all had failed, I could have gone with her or died with her. And in the days and months that followed, the number of ifs grew steadily, and these many years later, I still indulge in self-recriminations.

If she is dead, I have murdered her, as sure as God is my witness. I Gerhard Reichenberg, the honorable member of the Nazi party, had my hand in it. And I murdered my unborn child.

It's late now, Mr. Klein. The pain is getting unbearable. The nurse is bound to arrive any minute now with my medication. She'll barge in without knocking, the needle-tipped syringe pointing to the ceiling like a weapon to combat all ills. I hate that state of drug-induced sense of what they call "cloud nine." When it wears off, you just fall down to earth with a thud. But it does take away the pain. Perhaps that doping medication will help that other pain too, the one for which no one has yet invented a cure.

Respectfully yours,
Gerhard Reichenberg

I put the letter down, as yet undecided whether to feel more sorry for that Esta of his, for the unborn child, for all of us who had to live through it, condemned to witness it, condemned again to carry such memories for the rest of our lives, than for that man. I would like to feel sorry for him, but I still cannot. He stands there before me like those paintings on ancient Greek urns, of actors wearing two-faced masks that can be turned as the occasion calls for. One is Gerhard the crippled man desperately trying to hold on to his only leg, a leg that is dying and giving him pain, unbearable pain, he wrote, and that other pain, the different kind of pain, the kind I know so well. The other face is *Herr Reichenberg*, the elegant, overbearing, fear-inducing man of a long time ago. And they keep changing, one stepping forward in front of the other, then behind, and they take turns in that game of hide and seek, and they do so without rhyme or reason.

I wheel myself to the window. It's still raining. The sky is the color of wax paper. The vista is blurred by the steamy air inside. I raise the shutters and wipe away some of it, but the blur returns, and like a semitransparent curtain, it renders unreal all that is around me.

I try but cannot form a clear image of his Esta. So many Estas, Renatas, Channas, Manyas, Rivkas, dark-haired, dark-eyed, a blend of faces and voices. Crowded sidewalks, cracked stones, muddy streets on a day like that. A milling crowd, elbowing their way, jostling and vying for the little space there was. So few smiles, all of it painted with the brush of fear of men with swastikas, the weapons of murder at their side, the fence, the barbed wire. And that other kind of fear, the ill-defined, the kind that was there day and night like a debilitating fever.

Dusk, and I still sit at the window gazing at the past and at the present, the darkly outlined buildings housing so many, the lit rectangles with flickering lights. So many are blue, and as I watch closely, the lights become a cascade of colors. Television. I turn on mine and reluctantly watch the glorification of the young, the vigorous, the indestructible. I watch the young, the alluring, the unwrinkled, the shapely ones in the throes of faked passion or despair. I watch the agile skaters, the dervishes on the ice, inexhaustible, no pain in their hips. Arms, wing-like extensions of themselves, they soar weightlessly as if the laws of gravity pertained only to the likes of me or Gerhard lying there in his tent, probably doped up by that medicine they give him. And I watch those slender, caressing hands, the fingers like the tentacles of a graceful anemone, no knobby joints, no swollen knuckles the shape of play marbles. Ah, to be young again. Only for a single day. To be young and for a single night to bury my face in a woman's neck. Esther, my Esther, to possess and be possessed. One single night, one single gift of the gods.

Night has come, and I join the ranks of all the others behind those windows.

CHAPTER
13

Three days have gone by, and there still is no letter. Miss Hedberg, noticing me gaze at her pocket, shakes her head and shrugs. And like matchmakers all over the world, she too must be aware that once introduced, curiosity about each other rises with each exchange of missives. I can hear it in her self-satisfied tone of voice telling me about Gerhard.

"I saw him yesterday. He had a bad day, the nurse told me. His diabetes got out of control, and for a while, the poor man didn't know where he was and wanted to get out of bed and go into the garden for a walk. Imagine, go out in the rain and bitter cold."

We are on our way to my morning workout, and she continues. "He complained about pain, terrible, shooting pain, and he was pointing at the knee of his wooden prosthesis."

"You mean, he's up there?" I ask, making a circular motion with my finger over my temple. "You know, gone crazy?"

"No, no, Mr. Klein. It happens quite often to people who have lost a leg. Phantom pain, it's called. And no matter how hard you try to tell them, they insist that the pain is real, and they point to the bed sheets where there is nothing there. I had one man who insisted that his toes were hurting him beyond endurance, and he pointed at the place where his toes would have been, and there was no leg at all."

She must have sensed my concern because, patting me on the shoulder, she adds, "He was better today. This morning, I checked up on him, and he was wide awake. He even smiled back. And you know what he said, Mr. Klein?"

"No, tell me."

"He wanted to know if I delivered his last letter to you, and did you make any comments after you read it. Of course, I had to tell him that you did read it, and I was quite sure that you will write to him." She ends the sentence with a twinkle in her eyes.

She raises my leg and asks me to lower it all by myself.

"Miss Hedberg, you must be dreaming."

"Try, Mr. Klein, please?"

I try and nearly am able to do it.

"Well?" she asks with quizzically narrowed eyes.

"Well what?"

"You know what I mean, Mr. Klein. Will you write to him?

You know, I think right now a note from you would do him more good than that insulin and all the other drugs they give him."

"Yes, Doctor Hedberg."

"I'm not a doctor, Mr. Klein, I just know people. Will you write?"

"I promise."

"You're a good man, Mr. Klein. You're both good men."

Sunday. Visiting hours. Visitors come. I can hear them up and down the corridor, children's voices, small footsteps, and high-pitched chatter. A welcome diversion from the mundane. Robert and Margot are late again. I've learned to tolerate their hurried arrival, the dashing into my room short of breath as if they have run all the way. Today they are both excited.

"A new addition to the family," Margot announces with her usual advertising-poster smile, but this time it rings with a note of true joy. "We'll bring her home in …" She counts the number of days on her slender fingers. "In four days, and we wanted you to be the first to know."

"*Mazal tov.*" I wish them the customary Hebrew good luck, and for one brief moment, I too am carried on the wave of excitement. "An adoption, I suppose?"

"Well …" Margot hesitates for a brief moment. "The veterinarian says she's actually part of a litter; the others have been snatched away."

Margot is unstoppable now. "A basset hound, well not quite a little bit of a beagle but cute you should see her flapping ears and the cute white-tipped tail and you should have seen how she immediately took to Rob, you know all female dogs take to the men and ..."

I look at my son, and our eyes meet. He reads my disappointment and shrugs while Margot goes on about a name for the dog.

"Yes that's what we'll call her Eleanor you know after Mrs. Eleanor Roosevelt with the same hang-dog expression and puckered forehead or do you think it's being disrespectful with so many of our friends Democrats, and you know they still worship that woman although for the life of me I never could stand that high squeaky voice of hers ..."

We wait patiently for a hiatus between the unstoppable flow of words, and I finally raise my hand.

"Yes, Nathan?" She stops and looks at me reproachfully.

"I discovered an old acquaintance of mine, right here, in the other building." I nod at the steamed window.

"Isn't that wonderful, you found a friend?" Margot displays her pearly teeth. "Just the other day I said to Rob, 'Nathan is too much of a recluse and ought to get out of his shell and make an effort at meeting other people here, it would do him a lot of good,' didn't I, Rob?'"

"I said an acquaintance, not a friend. The man's name is

Gerhard Reichenberg. I used to know him many years ago, long before I arrived here. It was during the war."

I would like to continue, but my son, to preserve the sharp crease on his pants, tugs them up daintily before crossing his legs and then turns his hands palms down and goes on to inspect his fingernails. Margot nods her head and listens, but her eyes are off in some dream world about basset hounds that resemble Eleanor Roosevelt.

"Well anyhow, that was a long time ago." I continue. "And now, children, if you don't mind ..." I lean back in my chair, a sort of shorthand telling them it is time to leave.

And there is so much more I would like to tell them. And for so many years now.

Sunday, the 4th of December
Dear Mr. Reichenberg,

Visiting hours are over, and my son and daughter-in-law just left. I tried to tell them about you, but their minds were preoccupied with selecting a proper name for their dog.

Have you ever tried to confide some of what you wrote to me to your children? You never did get married, or did you? And if you did, were your children as disinterested in your past as my son, Robert, and his wife, Margot, are?

I wish I could help you in your search for that Esta of yours. You're not the only one still searching. Many of us of a background similar to mine, some living right here, others scattered all over the world, and after nearly one half of a century, they still keep searching. A symbolic kind of searching by reading through long rosters of participants in one kind of meeting of survivors or another. We know, without much doubt, what happened. And yet deep down our eyes are still riveted to long lists in search for a familiar name. Perhaps we do it only as a gesture of not having forgotten them. We all seem to have a need to erect a shrine to those we have lost, be it as modest as a simple earthen mound. It is our way of parting from one another, our epitaph to those we once loved and then lost irretrievably. Without it there lingers an added dimension of pain.

Ah yes, Gerhard, you too are raked by guilt of having survived while those whom you loved, your Esta and your unborn child, may have been killed. Welcome to the brotherhood of the guilty, the culpable, the self-proclaimed villains. Forgive me for being cynical, but for the longest time, I claimed that such guilt was the prerogative of us only. It was so overwhelming that I referred to it as the Holocaust survivor's malady, and in this we claimed to have a monopoly. But that was during the early years after the war. Since then, I grew wiser. And the longer I listened to the stories of surviving the more it became clear that guilt, that complex emotion, is made up of endless variations. A true kaleidoscope of the heart.

And the longer I listened to others and to myself the more I became aware that the cause of it was not that we survived while the lives of others had been snuffed out. That too played a role.

There was something else, something so forbidding that few dared to admit it, even to ourselves. We saw them die. That in itself was mind shattering. What really struck such forcible blow was watching and doing nothing to aid them. Silently, we witnessed events that no man had ever witnessed before, and all we did was weep. Silent and passive weepers, we were, so afraid and so anxious to live, if only for a while longer, that we even hid our tears for fear that it might draw the executioner's ire to us. At the time, it seemed the only thing one could do. But later on—ah yes, later on under the beguiling hindsight—but that is another story.

Strange how the chemistry in our brain keeps turning things upside down, to a point of having no resemblance to reality. You say you should have never left the ghetto when you did. You, the mighty Herr Reichenberg, before whom others cringed, you now believe that you could have saved her. I, Nathan, the apple of Mama's eye, on the day when they came for us, the little coward that I was, I ran out of the house without as much as glancing back at my parents, my brothers, my sister. How often have I asked myself, what if I had stayed behind? And it is here that this conjurer of conjurers enters and changes me into a man with the strength and courage of Hercules, a Samson fighting lions with his bare hands, and when all failed, in that last gasp of strength brings down the pagan temple and death to the enemy and himself. No end to our fantasies of what we could have done. Here lies buried the seed of our guilt, and there is no end to how much we punish ourselves for it.

Enough this wallowing in guilt for one night. You have problems now that need immediate attention. Miss Hedberg assures me that the doctor taking care of you is a good man and you are in the best of hands. Miss Hedberg divides the human race into good men and bad men. You and I are good men. Who knows, someday I might even start believing it.

Yours,
Nathan Klein

CHAPTER

14

Miss Hedberg arrives, a broad smile heralding the presence of a letter conspicuously sticking out of her pocket. She hands it to me with a gesture of pride and the look of *I told you so.* She nods at the letter and waits for me to open it. The envelope is thick, thicker than ever, almost bursting in its seams. To reciprocate, I take hold of it between the thumb and fingers of my clumsy left hand while I reach for the letter opener with my right. It's slow going, the letter slipping, yet I hold it firmly while her eyes follow my every move. Two letters are there, the pages of each held together by a paper clip.

"Bravo, Mr. Klein, you did it, and I knew you could." She silently claps her hands. "And just for that alone, I shall let you use the walker."

I haven't read the letter, but simply knowing that it's there makes my step more confident and self-assured. Going through the paces on the exercise couch, my limbs are less leaden.

Wednesday, the 7th of December
Dear Mr. Klein,

How thoughtful your letter. Guilt and remorse. How well you phrased it. But you left out the quest of forgiveness. I'm a religious person, a man of faith you could say, and if you believe in sin, you must also believe in redemption. Without the possibility to atone, guilt becomes a monstrosity no man could possibly endure. Prayer is God's gift to man, his way of forgiveness. And so I pray, but it doesn't seem enough.

The church, in the name of which so much wrong had been done to the Jewish people, and for such a long time now, seemed a hollow place to search for forgiveness. Something was forever telling me that whatever wrongs I may have committed in the eyes of God, those committed against man need the forgiveness of man. Now to you, Nathan the realist, the practical man who seems to have lost his belief in God, as you indicated in one of your first letters, this must sound pretentious if not outright stuffy. And I can imagine you shaking your head and finding this religiosity of mine incongruous with the Nazi emblem that I once wore so proudly on my left arm. This duality, one contradicting the other, in many ways has a lot to do with my upbringing. But of this some other time.

Let me just say that these same contradictions, although there *may have been many other things of which I'm only vaguely conscious, led me to the Nüremberg trials. It's a long story, the coming home from the war, a young man but no longer the youngster with all those harebrained vision of a Reich, a Deutsche Kultur, a Herrenrasse born to rule, and all that other clap-trap. I felt estranged in more ways than one and deeply disillusioned in all I had been taught to believe, and in all those who did the teaching. Home was a cold place. And I don't mean cold because part of the roof was missing and there was no money to buy fuel to heat the place. It was the chill of silence.*

Yes, at home we did speak to one another, but our language became an art of avoidance, a linguistic kind of tiptoeing around the war, of all that preceded it, the horrors of it, the occupation, and the news of all the atrocities committed by our men no matter where they ventured. And so many died, and so many came home crippled. Surprisingly, there was little weeping for them, as if the shedding of tears would be a sign of feeling sorry for what happened, a sign of regret and of repenting. The possible repercussions for what we, as a people, had done were never mentioned, nor were the concentration camps and prisons that were witnessed by so many. Instead we confined ourselves to such trivia as the meagerness of the ration cards, the cramped quarters, the black market, the looseness of our women who had taken up with the soldiers of the occupation forces. We became a nation of amnesiacs, it seemed, of men who came back dispirited and morose, some still wearing parts of their uniforms with POW stamped across their back.

But not forever. In time, the hungry bellies became filled, the nightmares of the battlefields ceased, and tongues loosened. For a while, I had come to believe that the war had changed us. Soon though, I was taken aback at seeing how many still longed for what they called the good days of the Kameradshaft, *that old, pernicious sense of oneness, ein* Volk, *ein* Führer, *and all that other nonsense.*

One of my neighbors, Johann Frohl, a strapping man just recently released from his war prison camp, returned home. I saw him coming down the street dressed in a Russian quilt jacket, oil and grease stained, full of holes with tufts of cotton sticking out, and crudely painted Russian markings of a prisoner of war in the back. His belongings in a simple sack slung over his shoulder. There he strode down the streets, grinning and waving at all his former neighbors like a conquering hero home from the front. I knew the man. He lived on the same floor. Last I saw him was during one of my furloughs home. By then he had risen to the rank of captain in some SS Panzer division, highly decorated for having fought on three fronts, the last on the Russian.

On the night of his arrival, his friends, all of them former warriors, gathered in his apartment to celebrate. A rowdy party at first, soon I could hear the man playing the piano. He was a fine musician, and there were many occasions before the war when we were invited, and he played for us. What struck me that evening was the music. He played Schubert's Lieder *and sang in his deep baritone. I listened to those wafting melodies I had heard so many* times. Through the wall separating his apartment from ours, I could only discern individual words. The Lieder was full of such lofty words as schönheit, blumen, frieden, ruhe—beauty, flowers, peace. So incongruous this, the man just having come back from years in a manmade hell, now playing those romantic songs about unrequited love and the longing for the sacred and the holy. And all this in a building, the walls pockmarked with shrapnel fragments, and the house next to it a pile of rubble and some of its occupants still unaccounted for.

I wondered if it was Johann singing or a gramophone record. I stepped into the corridor. The door to his apartment stood open, and I walked in. They were there, friends and neighbors, some still wearing army boots, pants, a worn army jacket. There they stood around the piano, wives, mothers, some wiping their eyes. They wept as the man sang, the same man who not long ago commandeered a tank and thought nothing of opening fire and mowing down men, women, children, anything that moved.

And then, just to change the pace, Johann stopped, smiled at those around him, and struck up a jaunty military song with the refrains of "Eins, zwei, und drei," and those around him took it up, clapping their hands in rhythm. With a snap of a finger, from the time it took to change from andante to allegro, they were back to the good old days of the Reich, as if nothing had happened.

Strange this mixture of lachrymose sentimentality and strident military tunes. This weaving in and out from the utterly romantic to the brutal and back again, as if we were all in possession of a dual personality, the devil with his cloven hoof, sprouting angelic wings and sporting a halo around his head. Misty-eyed gluttons for words and melancholy songs along with fire and brimstone.

I looked at them, at their gaiety in the midst of ruins, hardly a few months past an orgy of killings, and wondered which of these were the cold-blooded killers of so many, and perhaps of my Esta and her child too. I left. The door was wide open, and I found my father standing in the doorway. He too was caught up in the rhythm of that martial music. It was nauseating.

There were days of indecision, of floundering, not knowing whether I still belonged to these people I grew up with. Days of drifting toward becoming an outsider, of one that no longer belonged. A terrible feeling, this no longer belonging. Like standing naked on a crowded sidewalk with no place to hide and all the people fully dressed and staring at you.

I read the first issues of the recently opened Allgemeine Zeitung and learned of the Nüremberg trials. They opened officially on November 20, 1945. To me, the news was electrifying. They were putting on trial all these men I once worshipped and in time had come to despise. And I knew what they did. I saw the telltale of those deeds in all the gory details, deeds that needed to be told, deeds that should become known to the whole world, deeds perpetrated by the many that needed to be unmasked.

How naive I was in those days in my belief that I was one of the *few who witnessed it. Little did I know then that there were millions who were eyewitnesses to atrocities, the kind that not even I, so close to the scene, saw or heard of. But I needed to tell, to get it off my chest like a wounded man in search of someone to tend to his injury.*

The American Occupation Headquarters was located in the former I.G. Farben industry headquarters in my hometown, Frankfurt am Main. Perhaps they could steer me to the right place where I could speak out. I lived near the river. It was a long way, and I found myself getting off the jam-packed streetcar, people overflowing and hanging on with only one foot on the steps. I walked partway, stopping once in a while and wondering if this was the right thing to do. I sensed that this may well turn out to be the ultimate moment of separating myself from the man I once was.

My dear friend, allow me to stop here. This letter is much longer than I anticipated. Besides, unnerving as these recollections are, my head is tired, the medication is wearing off. In fact, all of me is wearing off, and I shall finish the letter tomorrow.

Gerhard

The next batch of pages is neatly held together by a paper clip, each page numbered, the handwriting more orderly than the last. He must have had a restful night.

Thursday, the 9th of December

Yesterday was a bad day. The doctor came, and for once the man didn't squeeze my shoulder and didn't proclaim with his all too familiar plural, "We're doing fine." Instead, he sat there near the edge of my bed and frowned, which was enough to send me into a state of panic. He then proceeded to explain to me that there were alternatives to just waiting for the circulation in my leg to improve using the medication they were giving me and all that other hocus-pocus. He said something about going under the knife, of doing some rerouting of the blood supply. He called it a bypass of one artery to another. But of course, he pointed out, there was always the risk of partial amputation. He then went on explaining the risk of just procrastinating and used the word gangrene. Gangrene, like a thunderbolt from a clear blue sky. I closed my eyes and bit down on my lips to stifle a cry of anguish. Little did the man realize the full meaning of that word. During war, gangrene was one more catastrophe word that went along with the numbing of limbs in a howling wind with little to shield one, then a while later realizing that ... But not now, dear friend. Let us not speak of it now. At any event, in the state I was, I couldn't understand half of it. What I need, now that I'm calmer, is for someone to explain it to me again.

You see, the thought of losing my one remaining leg was shattering. To have been bedridden with only occasional walks in the garden was painful enough, but I still had one good leg to stand on, even though at times even that seemed to rebel against me. There was the ever-present possibility that I might lose a toe or two. Better this than the entire leg. To be without legs was totally unacceptable. I *couldn't dwell on it, even for a second. I wouldn't let them. I'd rather lie here and wait for a miracle to happen. And don't ask me what that miracle might be.*

Here I go pouring out all my heartaches to you while you too must have had your days when only part of you remained under your control, the other rebelling against you. Miss Hedberg told me that you were getting better, and while I prayed for the salvation of my extremity, I took the liberty to include you in my prayer. I hope you don't mind.

Dear Mr. Klein,

I got sidetracked again, and yet I so wanted to finish the story of that time of one foolish twenty-eight-year-old man in a gesture of repentance and defiance trying to open the eyes of an entire world to what happened, not realizing that the whole world knew it down to each gory detail. I so wanted to speak up and tell of the many heartbreaking events I had witnessed.

I was shunted from one office to another until I found myself confronted by a young American lieutenant sitting behind a desk. There ensued a conversation, actually a whole string of them that I can never forget. To this day, I can vividly recall the faces, the intonations, the precise wording. It was a moment of utter humiliation.

I stated my name and all other personal data before I was even allowed to state the nature of my intent. I tried to speak English, but the young man insisted that I speak German. For a while, he listened patiently and then stopped me and, switching to his English, said, "Now, let's get this straight. Are you telling me that you have some information about war crimes, and you want to testify against the Germans who committed them?"

I assured him that this was precisely why I was there.

"And you are telling me that you are a German and not one of those DPs, you know, Displaced Persons?"

I nodded my head. "Yes, sir," I said. "I'm a German and a former member of the NSDP."

"NSDP. And what does that stand for?"

"I was a former Nazi, sir," I said, trying to be as calm as possible.

His eyes bulged. The young woman, a secretary sitting at another desk alongside the wall, ceased typing.

"Holy shit," he exclaimed. "I'll be a son of a bitch!" He let his pen fall down on the desk. "This has got to be a first."

He rose. "Here, sit down." He nodded at one of the chairs near the secretary's desk. "I'll be back in a jiffy."

He left through a connecting door to an adjoining office. The door ajar, I could hear the man conversing with another official, much of it unintelligible, but I did hear the word "ratting." It was only later that I realized that ratting pertained to being a traitor, a stool pigeon.

As I sat there waiting for the outcome of that unsavory interview, the true light of my action was brought home to me by the young woman. She was German, and her accent placed her clearly in my city. Once again, she stopped her work at the typewriter.

"Sind sie wirklich ein Deutscher?" *Are you truly a German?* she asked with a note of disbelief, first glancing at the door and making sure we were not being overheard.

Anger was welling up inside me, and it must have shown on my face, for the young woman slowly shook her head and then yanked out the sheet of paper from the typewriter, crumpled it several times, and threw it into basket near her feet. The gesture left no doubt of its meaning. Garbage. In her eyes, I was garbage.

After that, few things seemed to matter. I was told to speak to the man in the next office. More formal and reserved, he bid me to sit, offered me a cigarette, and after I refused flicked a stick of chewing gum from a pack that I also declined. It was a series of interviews, some with an official alone, others in the presence of a stenographer, some in my halting English, some in German, the last one in the presence of a distinguished, older man in civilian clothes whose name was Mr. Robertson, but it could have been Robinson.

He thanked me. At first, he kept asking repeatedly if I was ever demoted from the ranks. Was I by any chance a member of an anti-Nazi underground? Was I ever arrested, beaten, or tortured? Addressing me as "young man," he made quite a speech about wishing there were more like me, about fortitude, courage, coming face to face with what really happened. He went on and on, and I soon realized that the man was speaking less to me than to the others in the room, *stenographers, interpreters, and to one who introduced himself as being from the* Stars and Stripes, *a reporter for the occupation newspaper who kept scribbling rapidly, stopping Robertson once in a while with a raised hand. Later on, I read that Robertson was an expert on international law and a well-known member of the judiciary.*

I was let go and told that I might be called upon to testify by deposition either here in Frankfurt or in Nüremberg but would be informed so by letter. In the meantime, I should try not to leave the city unless on urgent matters.

I gave them my home address, the only one I could think of without suspecting to what degree that single misstep would change my entire life.

On the long downhill walk to the nearest streetcar stop, the imposing building looming behind me, I kept on reliving my interviews. My head was in turmoil. The last few traces of feeling heroic about going to the Americans had vanished. I felt like a traitor, a renegade, a man who had turned against his own, and this at a time when all around us lay in ruin and most of my fellow countrymen were desperate to pick up the pieces and go on with their lives. No one said openly that I was a traitor while being questioned, not outright. But it was there, in their voices, in their exchange of glances with each other, in that crumpled sheet of paper thrown into a wastebasket with such wrath, and in that patronizing way the old man Robertson was lecturing about conscience, rectitude, and some other highfalutin' stuff.

Don't get me wrong; they were polite, these many men who kept asking the same questions as if wanting to see if they could trip me on some inconsistencies until I began to feel like a criminal under interrogation. And there were moments when they succeeded—I began feeling like a criminal, not so much for what I had done but for what we Germans had done, and I, the sole culprit of all the misdeeds committed, these same misdeeds I came to reveal.

How strange it felt being there, the imposing staircase, the long corridors with numerous doors, people, most of them in uniform, and I in my shabby civilian suit, one I hadn't worn for a long time and was now ill-fitting. I felt threadbare and unkempt among them, reduced in size, dwarfed. And yet none of those going about their business deigned to look at me. The few that did cast a glance did so in the perfunctory manner of officialdom. I became acutely aware of the one profound difference between all those around me and myself. They wore a uniform. That symbol of power that elevates a man above the ordinary, the mundane. And it gives the bearer a sense of being superior to all the others.

How well I knew that feeling.

In their eyes, I felt, I was just one more German, a Kraut, a Hun, not a man torn by the kind of anguish none of them could possibly fathom. As I look back, this was the way we all must have gazed at the Jews, the Poles, the Russians, and all the other people in countries that were ours for just the taking. And we inspired fear. You wrote about it, calling me the Herr Arbeitsleiter, powerful and invincible, someone to fear and to obey.

It was many months later that I learned of having been one of the few, a handful only, that volunteered to testify. Ah yes, there was of course Kurt Gerstein. A tragic figure of a man, also a former member of the Nazi party, but a man who placed himself in the opposition quite early and suffered all the inequities the Reich meted out to anyone opposed to them—prison, concentration camps, and so on. Having volunteered to join the Waffen-SS and having witnessed the worst of all excesses of the Reich, the goings on in the extermination camps, he set out to tell, to stir the world conscience. Quite unsuccessfully, as it turned out. Poor man. At war's end, the French arrested him as a war criminal. They say the man was murdered by his SS fellow inmates. Others claimed that he committed suicide out of despair of wanting to warn the world and having no one listen. It took another twenty years before someone wrote a play about him, The Deputy. Poor man.

I read the play. How well I understood that man, Gerstein. Too well, I'm afraid.

God! Nearly three pages, and I only intended to put a finish to my last letter. I could go on and on. The older I get, the more garrulous I become. Is it age? Perhaps. But it could also be the storing up of so many things I wanted to tell for so long now, and no one wanting to listen. Or is it a need to tell before it's too late? And of all the people to whom I finally bare my innermost thoughts, it has to be you, Mr. Klein?

Cordially yours,
Gerhard Reichenberg

CHAPTER
15

The food on my tray has grown cold, and I'm still writing, possessed by an uncontrollable urge to say all that I feel before the day comes to an end, before all that surges through my head takes flight. He too, *Reichenberg*, speaks of sorrow, sadness, fear. It's all there in the many pages now scattered on the table, neatly numbered in his orderly way. I look at them, and I can see the man through the lines. The *Her Arbeitsleiter*, the once powerful and invincible Herculean man with his strident gait, turns into a crippled, old man.

Friday, the 10th of December
Dear Mr. Reichenberg,

And so I committed the unpardonable sin of lumping all men into neat categories, labeling them and stashing them away into the endless numbers of compartments in my brain. In my mind, you were a thug, an ordinary hoodlum clad in an ideology proclaiming you to be superior to all other men and furnishing you with a license to kill and to rob all those that displeased you. In a nutshell, you were a Nazi. And so I kept seeing you for the better part of these fifty years.

I still haven't been able to change my mind. That you were. A hoodlum and a Nazi. But it seems you were a hoodlum with a bit of heart. A pity it lay dormant for so long and that it took a Jewish maiden in the form of a bribe to make that heart of yours beat with a human rhythm. I don't believe that this was the intent of the Jews in the ghetto. They were not that clever, nor did they give a damn about your morals; they had enough problems keeping their own from going haywire. As you realized, she was meant to be simply a greasing of the palm, as they say, someone to soften you up, so that when the time came you'd be less inclined to do us harm.

How sad your story. Less strange to me, having listened to so many others. But then you were a strange man to start with. You claim to have been one of the few Germans, former party members who came forward to testify against your own people. I often wondered why so few spoke up among the many who had the ringside seats in that macabre show of butchery. The war over, all I could see were crestfallen faces, pious voices of your fellow Germans who claimed not to have had the slightest inkling of what was being done to millions. Most of the stories were oozing with self-pity. To us, who managed to survive, that claiming of innocence of yours was the closest to being just so many cruel jokes.

You wrote about the trials, and you touched on the subject of uniforms. I followed those trials as if I had been the one sitting in judgment over these men in the dock. I remember listening to the American radio broadcasts and looking at the pictures in the Stars and Stripes, overjoyed at the sight of the courtroom and all these men sitting in the dock with earphones on their heads, some listening intently, some not listening at all, defiantly staring down at the floor or up at the ceiling. Without their uniforms, every one of them looked like just ordinary muggers in a police lineup. You're right about uniforms. Let me add, uniforms can also degrade, especially those with black and white stripes, the kind so many of us were compelled to wear, and for so long.

I remember those trials well; international headliners they were for weeks and months. Justice at last. But how short our memories. Two generations since those events took place, and our young men of today are more familiar with names like John Lennon, Bruce Springsteen, and Mick Jagger than with names like Goebbels, Himmler, Eichmann, and other cutthroats, men who came close to ruling the world.

Before I finish reminiscing about those trial days, let me comment on one aspect that at the time rankled me more than it does today. The judges were Americans, Englishmen, Frenchmen, and Russians. I would have preferred to have seen German judges, Germans sitting *in judgment of their own, and of course, German witnesses of the likes of you enumerating the enormity of the crimes committed. Mea culpa, mea maxima culpa—how conspicuously absent that was. I would have liked to see Germans meting out the punishments, Germans building the gallows, and Germans pulling the lever to spring the trap doors while the German public at large applauded. But no, others had to come to bring down that charnel house, and others sat in judgment and meted out the punishment. It somehow grated on my sense of justice. It still does. But having come face to face with the likes of you ... well, let's say it makes me feel better to learn that there were some who at the time felt the same way. Even if there were only a few, as you claim.*

And so you're still searching for her. How tempted I am to put an end to that tragic story of yours by telling you that, yes, I knew Esta, that she was a distant cousin of mine, that indeed she did hide and by some miracle managed to survive, and the last I saw her, she was a happy woman standing at the dockside in Naples, her suitcases at her feet, a beautiful child in her arms, waiting to board a ship taking them to Palestine. How it tempts my hand to invent such a lie just so I could put a happy ending to that wounded life of yours. But I'm Nathan, a stranger to happy endings, and as much as I would like to write that down, I must tell you that I don't know what happened to her.

Somewhere in one of your letters, you did mention something about having gone to Jerusalem in search for her. I too have visited that city, although for a different reason, and I would like to hear your impression of it. As a youngster, still a believer in a God merciful and just, Jerusalem was part of my frequent prayers. My impression of the city would likely be diametrically opposite of yours. But who knows? You are a Christian, a religious man, and as such, you inherited from us the saga of that city, the temple, the Mount of Olives, and all the other trappings of your faith. Speaking of religion, a God-fearing Nazi in search of redemption in Jerusalem—it has to be another one of those contradictions of terms.

I'm being sarcastic, Gerhard. I know. But being sarcastic is only one of my minor character flaws. Wait till you get to know some of my others.

Sorry to hear about your leg. I know the agonies of becoming crippled. Even during the most despairing moments of waking up and realizing that I had no control over my left side, I still had hope of regaining it, tenuous at times, but there it was. I could look at my leg, at my arm, my hand, I could make an effort to infuse life into them, but what you are facing carries such finality.

Of course, there was also my profession. I don't remember now if I wrote to you—I'm a watchmaker. Or I was one. Can you see a watchmaker with only one useful hand? I don't know what you do for a living. Perhaps you are a man who sits all day, a bookworm of some kind, perhaps a writer, or an accountant, but to me, the loss of function of one hand would be disaster.

And now comes the skeptic. I'm an old man with an overblown sense of distrust of one and all. Are you sure you have the best of doctors? I have learned to distrust them. They too are only human with the shortcomings we all have. They make errors in judgment, like you and I, and with the best of intentions. What you face may be too important to leave to the judgment of one man. What I'm trying to tell you—get another opinion.

We hardly know each other, and here I go meddling in your affairs.

It's been ages since I wrote letters this long. When it comes to being talkative, we seem to be echoing each other. Something tells me we have a lot more to say to each other than I thought.

Yours,
Nathan Klein

P.S. I scanned the letter once more before sealing it. How self-righteous and sanctimonious I sound. Sorry about that.

CHAPTER
16

Miss Hedberg barges in. Her eyes are downcast. Her pocket is empty.

"They took him. Early this morning, the ambulance came, and they took him." She bursts out in tears. "Someone should have had the decency to tell me." She looks at her watch impatiently, and seeing me gaze at the wheelchair, she hastens to add, "Ja, ja, so you want to use the walker. Like little children. Once they learn to walk, they'll never crawl again." She is clearly on edge this morning, her gestures abrupt and her voice brusque. She opens the door and impatiently waits for me to shift my weight and find my balance. This morning, the walk down the corridor is arduous, and we precede slowly, my eyes riveted to the floor and on the tips of my walker. Tight-lipped, she walks a few paces behind me.

"Not a word, mind you," she says, finally breaking the silence.

"This morning, I came into his room just to say good morning, and what do I find?" She raises both hands. "An empty bed. Only a mattress. The closet door open, and his clothes are gone. You know, Mr. Klein, my heart stopped beating. I thought, *Poor Gerhard, something must have happened to him during the night, a heart attack or some other dreadful thing, and he died.*"

One by one, she relates the events of last night. Gerhard, according to the nurse, became agitated in the middle of the night and called for the nurse. Quiet at first, he soon screamed at the top of his voice, and the nurse came running in. He had pulled away the bed sheets, ripped away the tent, and holding to his leg kept half-screaming, half-crying, "My leg! I cannot feel my leg! Nothing down there below my knee! It's all gone! Someone help me, please!" They called for the doctor, and by the time he arrived, the leg had gone cold.

"They rushed him into the hospital, and you know, Mr. Klein, the doctor didn't even bother to tell us what they intend to do to him.

"Poor Gerhard." Her voice has become nasal. Angrily, she reaches into her pocket for a tissue, and in so doing, a small envelope falls to the ground. She bends down and hands it to me.

"Sorry about that, Mr. Klein. I'm so upset this morning, I nearly forgot. The nurse gave it to me and said something about a letter left lying on the pillow. It's so unfair to take him like this without telling a soul."

I look at the envelope. Smaller than his usual stationary and addressed to Miss Ulrica Hedberg, and bracketed in smaller letters, c/o Mr. Nathan Klein.

Miss Hedberg stops flexing and extending my arm and looks at me expectantly. The letter still sealed, I look at her, and she nods, bidding me to go ahead. A single sheet of paper, no date, the words hastily written. Miss Hedberg steps to the head of the couch and reads over my shoulder.

Dear Mr. Klein,

I awoke with pain in my leg, the kind of pain even the painkiller medicine didn't touch. Well, maybe just a little. The doctor came by, examined me hastily, sleep still in his eyes, and told me that I may need surgery and time is of essence now. I asked him what he intended to do, and he said something about not being sure until I get transferred to the General Hospital and have some tests done. I wanted to know how soon, and he replied that any minute counts now. The ambulance is on the way. A brief note just in case I may not have the opportunity to write again. I thank you for all your kindness these past few weeks. There was pain, and there was joy. Much, much more joy than pain in seeing that something is being done at last, instead of this dreary waiting for so long now. I have hastily tied together three folders containing some documents you may find of interest. I would like you to have them, and of course, in the top folder are your letters. These I consider intimate communications, some of the most cherished I have ever received, and they must not fall into the hands of those who may not understand them. There is a wooden box on my desk. My tools. My most cherished possession. I would like you to keep them safe until I get back and should I …

Excuse me for stopping here, but I can hear the wailing sound of the ambulance, and if I'm not mistaken, it's for me. Ah, here is the nurse.

Yours,
Gerhard

Miss Hedberg sniffles now. I turn to look at her red eyes, and she forces a smile through her tears, much of her face concealed by the crumpled tissue she uses to wipe her eyes.

"Poor Gerhard. One of the nicest patients here—a kind man, refined, and always so polite." She blows her nose and stashes the tissue into her pocket. For one fleeting moment, I am tempted to make some comment about her description of Gerhard as to that "kind, refined, and always polite man," especially about the "always," but this is neither the time nor the place to speak ill of him.

"I hope they can save his leg." She clears her throat. "And you know, in the way he was writing to you each time I came to see him, he was very fond of you, Mr. Klein."

"Let's not use the past tense, Miss Hedberg. For all I know, he is alive, and in time they'll ship him back here."

"You're right, Mr. Klein." She resumes exercising my limbs. "And you know what? I may go and visit him, and if you want to, you could …"

"Yes, Miss Hedberg, I'd like to write to him."

Noon time. The usual clanging noises of food carts and trays break the stillness of the place. Miss Hedberg delivers the box, placing it reverently right next to my cup holding an assortment of pens and pencils, a not-too-subtle reminder to write to her Gerhard.

"Sorry about those folders," she adds. "They were gone by the time I got back to his room. The nurse on duty told me that all his belongings had been placed in storage down in the basement and cannot be released without a patient's written permission, or, as the case may be, by his relatives or a court order.

"Now, as soon as I find out what happened, I'll be back to tell you."

Gerhard is alive. The last few days of waiting for Miss Hedberg to bring some news of him have been filled with an uneasy anticipation. The news about him is sketchy. They rushed him to the General Hospital in the early morning hours and took him straight to the operating room. They did some complicated artery to artery hook-up, but it is as yet too early to say how successful it was in saving his leg. Miss Hedberg bubbles over with excitement.

"Just think." Having dashed in hurriedly, she speaks in halting sentences, short of breath. "He came out of surgery. Alive, he is, and talking. Mumbles, in German. Three long hours of surgery. And at his age."

I find myself carried on the wings of her excitement as she pokes her head in to tell me that his leg is warmer now. "And God willing, Gerhard will be with us in no time." She raises her eyes to the ceiling. "And God, I never prayed so hard in my whole life."

CHAPTER
17

THICK SNOWFLAKES LAND ON the windowpanes and are quickly washed away by rain. I suddenly feel cold even though the old radiator is pinging away, the same inner cold I woke up to the day I arrived here and felt alone. I try to read, but letters and lines melt as quickly as the snowflakes. I shift my gaze to the opaque window. Not wanting to, I miss the man. I miss that calligraphy of his, and I miss my ritual of gazing out the window, wondering if the bench is empty.

Ten days have gone by and still no letter. Miss Hedberg, matchmaker, mailman, lately the carrier of messages traveling from nurse to nurse, to her, to me, informs me that his diabetes had gone out of control, and they have to keep the man in the hospital longer than they anticipated. I open the toolbox once again. There inside, Gerhard conveys another facet of himself. His tools are there, meticulously wrapped in a chemise cloth—chisels, borers, sharp knives, honed and oily to the touch, each one in its own compartment—a woodcarver's tools. I must ask him what these are for. His prized possession, he said. A thug with a heart, and now it seems a thug with an artistic bend. I must do it before it's too late.

His letter arrives by mail, a bulging envelope, the flap reinforced with Scotch tape. I rip it open, afraid that these are some of the old documents he described in his last note. But they are his recent handwriting, the pages meticulously numbered. Elated, I thumb through them. "Dear Nathan," "Dear Friend"—a few weeks ago, I would have found them too forward and too intimate, but now they somehow seem to fit the tenor of our evolving relationship.

Tuesday, the 14th of December
Dear Friend,

> *Hurrah! Hallelujah! Thank God!*
> *I would like to shout, giggle, sing. They saved it, Nathan, they did. I would like to get out of bed and dance—yes, on the one leg I still have, and now, it seems, a good one. And I would like to hug that young whipper-snapper of a surgeon who looks like a high school kid, with his sheepish grin, his pimples, and all. And I would like to get down and kneel on that leg and pray. There is something to praying on your knees. I don't know why; it must have something to do with being a child and having to kneel at the side of my bed before being allowed to hop in and go to sleep.*

The leg is warm, the pain is gone—well, nearly gone. It has been such a long time now since I felt like I won something. In that lifelong ledger of gains and losses, the column of gains is so small. Ever felt like hugging your own leg? Silly, isn't it?

I wanted to write to you sooner, but the anesthesia and some other medication they gave me made me feel all muddled. My head felt empty, and shaking it, I hoped to hear something rattle in there like coins in a piggy bank. I tried to write, twice in fact, but fell asleep in the middle of a sentence, and when I awoke, the things I had written made no sense at all, so I tore it up.

I don't know when this letter will reach you, but the first occasion I get, I shall ask the nurse to mail it. A lovely young woman, dark hair and large, dark eyes, but nowhere as beautiful as … Dear God, will I ever stop searching?

I have your last letter with me. I grabbed it to take it with me just as they so unceremoniously yanked me out of bed and rushed me into this hospital here. I read it and reread it. It has been a sustenance. I owe you answers to the many questions you have asked, and there are many more that beg telling you. But not yet. I'm well, not quite well though. They say I have a touch of pneumonia, but I wanted you to know what is happening.

Oh, oh, here they come again with a gurney, and I think this one is meant for me to go down to have some more x-rays taken or something like that.

Gerhard

Friday, the 17th of December
Dear Nathan,

To my chagrin, I found my last letter still in the drawer of my bedside table, yet I distinctly remember having left it on top and asking the nurse to mail it. Or did I? Things are still muddled, and today, to make matters worse, I have a fever. Cold, shivering one minute, then hot and perspiring, and my chest hurts each time I try to take a deep breath. Pneumonia—a dying man's friend, I read somewhere, a compassionate bon voyage into the next realm.

I share a room with one other patient. A sick man, though I have no idea what ails him. Sometime today, or was it during the night, he ceased moaning, and I believe he lapsed into a coma. He has visitors, and they are clearly family, one of them calling him over and over again, "Papa, can you hear me?" They are at his bedside with the curtains drawn all around—must be some sort of vigil. Poor man. Once in a while, I catch a glimpse of those sorrowful faces, one woman in particular, her eyes swollen and a handkerchief crumpled in her fist. At times, I wish that once in a while, especially during visiting hours, my curtain would part, and some familiar voice would greet me. Will there be someone at my bedside when the end comes? Morbid thoughts, I know. But hospitals like this are morbid places.

I cannot wait to go back to our place, to Miss Hedberg, to the garden with the gravely path, the few flowers, and my bench. It must be snowing now. I never thought that I would be missing a place where most people are sent to spend the last days of their lives.

Yours,
Gerhard

The next two pages are stuck to each other, probably some food stuff, and I have to use my pen knife to pry them apart.

Saturday, the 18th of December
Dear Nathan,

I reached into the drawer, and my letters to you are still there. If they hadn't taken away my artificial leg and cane, I would have hobbled toward the nurse's station to see that they were mailed. Tomorrow morning, that young doctor I mentioned before is liable to make rounds, and I will ask him. He's a decent kind, but I wish he would cease saying, "And how are we today, Pops?" It's a bit undignified, this "Pops," don't you think so? Especially by one so young. But considering what he has done for me, he is forgiven.

I hope you received my folder with some of the documents I left for you. There is one in particular I wanted you to have. It was written to me by some young man (I think he was young) from the office investigating war crimes. It was a personal letter from one of the many men who interviewed me on the day I so fool heartedly went to volunteer information, "to tell it all," as they say. Feldheim was his name. Lieutenant Saul Feldheim. If you haven't read it yet, someday when I get back, I hope to tell you all about it.

It was one of those fateful letters that unintentionally influenced the course of my entire life. Not the content, mind you. It was simply the arrival at my house as a letter written to me, the stationary, an official United States government envelope. My parents, the first ones to set eyes on it, must have speculated on its content and discussed it long before I returned home in the evening after having spent another day in futile search for work.

"That came for you, Gerhard." My father nodded at the unopened letter leaning against the salt shaker in the center of the kitchen table, our customary place to eat. It was his voice, with its clearly pretended casualness, and my mother's eyes boring into me with her look of anticipating another quarrel between him and me that told me how much importance they placed on a letter from the Amis—the name for Americans in those days. I opened it and read it while none of us touched the food. It was a brief, personal note to thank me for having volunteered to testify. His distant relatives lived somewhere in Eastern Poland and perished. He wondered if I ever came across a town that sounded like Kapol, or it could have been Topol, he wasn't sure. My parents' eyes were riveted on me while I scanned the letter, and there was no way I could conceal its nature.

So I told them. I thought I could tell it simply, like others who came home at war's end and spoke casually of some of the things that happened to them in a manner of getting things off their chest.

Or the way my father spoke of his war in the trenches somewhere in France, or was it Belgium during World War One. But I couldn't speak about it without alluding to some of the reasons that made me go to the Americans in the first place. There was clearly anger and bitterness in my voice. I spoke of the ghetto, the hunger, the atrocities committed there, and lastly of Esta and the child. I heard myself stumbling, words tripping each other, long pauses between sentences. My throat was constricted, the food in front of me untouched, my father staring at me with eyes that seemed to have become like two icicles. They just sat there and listened and asked no questions.

It's a long story, Nathan. My father never spoke to me again. My mother wept each time I broached the subject. For a while, I was foolish enough to believe that what made them turn against me was Esta and the unborn child, and what they may have construed as my desertion of her at a time she needed me. But I was wrong, Nathan. So wrong.

"How could you have done this to him, Gerhard?" my mother said a few days later. "You, his only son, his only hope to carry on the Reichenberg family name and, mit einer Polnishen Jüdin?—with a Polish Jewess? And then to make matters worse, you went to the Amis to tell on your own people?" Denunzieren—informing, was the word she used.

I never did find out which of the two crimes were the more odious in their eyes. Was it the fathering of a Jewish child, the mother eine Jüdin, or the volunteering to be a witness at the trial of war criminals? I never bothered to ask my father and mother what it was that so tormented them, for there was more to come. They were not the only ones who turned against me. Like a contagion, it was—a pestilence that starts with the illness of one and then spreads to infect all the others. At first, it was only the immediate family, aunts, cousins, and so on, then the neighbors, and in the end the entire street, and eventually, after I found employment, the workplace.

And by the way, they never did call on me to testify. Small fry, as they say here. Compared to all the other brutalities, what I had to contribute was only a trifle, nothing worth making a note of.

It's a long story, Nathan. I'm getting tired. Let me just end it here by saying that I became the social outcast, a renegade. And they were unforgiving in their judgment. The old standards of moral conduct of that pernicious creed of the Reich still prevailed: Die Fahnen hoch, die Reihen fest geschlossen—*standards aflutter, the ranks are firmly closed.* The old Nazi marching song still echoed in their ears.

Our Gerhard and a Jewess—a sin beyond forgiveness and without possibility of appeal. I left the country and came here.

Yours,
Gerhard

P.S. I could sleep forever and still be tired.

Miss Hedberg is delighted. I show her the many pages, and she touches them, smiling, as if touching his letters is touching him. I tell her the good news, and she claps and raises herself on her tiptoes like a child with a new toy. She frowns as I tell her of his pneumonia.

"That's dreadful, Mr. Klein. So many survive their operation only to … well, you know what I mean. But he is strong, and he will make it. I have a good instinct for such things. Besides, I will also pray for him."

I nod my head in agreement, and she quickly adds, "I pray for you too, Mr. Klein. Every morning, I pray for the two of you. Really, Mr. Klein, I do."

She promises to see to it that from now on his letters are mailed promptly. "Trust me, Mr. Klein. I know many people here and at the General Hospital. I used to work there at one time."

Monday, the 20th of December
Dear Gerhard,

Good news—bad news. But mostly good news to be cheerful about. Your leg—what better news could you wish for? Sorry about that pneumonia thing. Miss Hedberg assures me that she prays for you every morning, and according to her, prayer works better than all the medicines in the world. I wish I could believe that.

How sad that story of being rejected by your family and friends. Sad for you, sad for the many countrymen of yours still trapped in the past and looking back at the pages of history, sad for all of us. I used the plural, "the many countrymen of yours," and in so doing, I committed the sin of lumping together an entire people. I was told that in the beginning there were many who were opposed to some of that insanity, but they were swept aside, many silenced forever.

They claim that a new generation, actually two, grew up since that thuggery had its sway, and it's only recently that they have come to face the past. I watched television with utter amazement how tens of thousands, or was it hundreds of thousands, mostly the young, marched in protest through the streets of some major city. They walked solemnly, and I believe silently, carrying lit candles in glass cups, sadness etched in their faces. No strutting like their grandfathers. They just walked, and out of step. They were mourning and walking in protest against the wanton killings of foreigners, Turks, I believe. What a far cry from those torch parades and the singing, "heute gehört uns Deutschland und morgen die ganze Welt ..." Today it is Germany, tomorrow the whole world. Let us hope that the past never rears its ugly head again. Let me add here that I was struck by the absence of old faces in that crowd. I suppose we oldsters don't readily take to the streets, no matter what the cause. Could it be that at our ages we are too mired in the past to face the present?

I never did get your folders. You must tell me all about it once you're back here.

The snow is falling but immediately turns into a soggy slush. There is hammering all over the place—gives me a headache.

They're getting ready to celebrate Christmas. The other day, in the spirit of fairness and evenhandedness, a Rabbi poked his head in the door, wanting to know if I wish to participate in the lighting of the Chanukah candles. Before I even shook my head, the man said, "I know, I know what you'll say, but I have to ask just the same." And then he shrugged and raised his hands. "Who knows? Maybe you'll change your mind. I've seen it happen before, you know."

In any event, should you fail to be back by then, I wish you a Merry Christmas.

Yours,
Nathan

CHAPTER
18

Miss Hedberg arrives dressed as Santa Claus. Red hat with a white fur trimming, oversized pants, trousers stashed inside rubber boots, belt and bulging midriff, cotton tufts pasted to her jaws and eyebrows, rouge on her cheeks, and a heavy layer of lipstick making her look half-Santa, half-clown. Slung over her shoulder is a large canvas bag with red and white bunting, the bag bulging with neatly wrapped and beribboned packages. I hand her a Christmas card addressed to her with a few inane wishes I scribbled on it. I did it with my left hand, the letters printed clumsily. She spots it immediately and puts her arm around my shoulders.

"How wonderful, Mr. Klein. The best present you could have given me. And I didn't even teach you to do that. And now, Mr. Klein, for having been an extra good boy all year, I have something for you, sir."

With a pretended frown, she goes on rummaging through her bag. "Now, where is that extraspecial present someone very nice has asked me to deliver?"

I unwrap the package clumsily while she watches over my shoulder. A small package tied with a large ribbon, from G. R. written in his handwriting. I shake it, and it doesn't rattle. Inside, wrapped in fine tissue, is a carved ivory letter opener, the carving a series of decreasingly smaller elephants, trunk to tail all the way from the hilt of the silver handle to the tip. The aged ivory is a deep yellow, and the silver handle is tarnished. Clearly an antique, probably expensive. Folded is Gerhard's note.

Dear Nathan,

You may not be accustomed to receiving presents at Christmas time, but I happen to be in the habit of giving them. So please accept it with my best wishes.

Yours,
Gerhard

I'm deeply moved.

"Typical Gerhard," Miss Hedberg says. "Well, I better go on." She blows her nose into her handkerchief, an all too familiar prelude to her eyes brimming with tears. She closes the door quietly in sharp contrast to the rambunctious entry a short while ago.

The snow keeps falling. I hear the sound of bells in some far-off corridor and the opening and closing of many doors. There must be other Santas making their rounds. Tinny voices sing a Christmas carol, too perfect the singing, and too high pitched, more like a boys' choir, probably the radio or television. I'm averse to celebrating Christmas with all that Christ holiness, the robed priests, the inner sanctum of the candle-lit church, the cross, many crosses. A throwback to where I come from and who I am. But here it is all around me; it inundates me, together with all those colorful packages in Miss Hedberg's cornucopia bag. The many lights in those windows now twinkle at me, and I finally succumb and simply gaze at them and listen to the lachrymose voice of Bing Crosby.

Monday, the 3rd of January
Dear Gerhard,

A happy New Year to you. Miss Hedberg, our Hermes, that untiring messenger of the gods, keeps me abreast of your illness. So you had a setback. Your leg is fine, she tells me, but your lung infection got out of control, and it had something to do with your diabetes. And while I was watching the brightly lit Time Square, the apple slowly dropping and the crowds cheering ecstatically, you were drugged, out there in some astral space, and missed the old year becoming history and the new one a carte blanche waiting to be written on.

You didn't miss a lot. The old year was not all that good to be sending it off with a heartfelt good-bye. And the way things are shaping up in the world at large, the new year bodes even worse. Someone with a sense of the macabre counted the numbers of wars on this planet Earth of ours during the past year. Twenty-seven. And it was printed somewhere on the back pages of the newspaper between an article predicting a new earthquake in the Pacific Ocean and one dealing with the rapid proliferation of the dingo, those wild dogs in Australia, and their threat to the livestock in their outback.

But you feel better, she tells me.

Not much is happening here. I looked at the old calendar and was amazed at the many blank spaces. I'm a devoted calendar scribbler. If a day goes by, and there is nothing for me to make a note of, I consider it a loss, a day gone by in vain, a pebble fallen into the sea, and I feel guilty for having wasted it in idleness.

Not wanting to be outdone by you, I asked my son to bring me my old toolbox. It stands next to yours now. Mine is a simple shoebox, the sides torn and held together with tape. There it is on the table next to your oak, or whatever polished wood yours is made of, with brass hinges and a hasp to keep it locked. If toolboxes are to be measures of our characters, I ought to hide mine. And I don't mean the toolbox.

I think I wrote to you about being a watchmaker. Retired, of course, but still tinkering here and then. My fascination with watches goes way back to my childhood. While other youngsters were playing marbles or whittling, I would stand in front of a clock and watch the pendulum go back and forth, the sound of the chime being sheer joy to my ears.

And that's what I ended up doing for a living. Or did, for nearly a lifetime until this stroke. Nothing fancy. Just a plain, ordinary watchmaker. I repaired them, sold them, appraised them, and on the side dabbled in jewelry. Most people think that looking into the inside of a little thing like a watch must be the dullest occupation in the world. Not so, my friend. It takes good eyes and a lot of patience.

And let me add, you get to be a good psychologist. You'd be surprised how attached some people can get to a watch, even if it's nothing more than a piece of junk not even worth the effort to throw it away. But they go on wearing it day and night. Some shine in the dark like a beacon; night and silence all around them, they place it to their ears—tick-tock—it speaks to them. Or, if they wake up from a bad dream or whatever, it tells them that all is well, that there are hours of good sleep ahead and nothing to be afraid of.

It's a timepiece, a timekeeper, and as such, it brings order into chaos. The lover stands on a corner, and if his date is late, he looks impatiently at his watch. The doctor looks at the clock to register the moment of birth, and the nurse does the same when the patient has taken his last gasp, and they write it down to the exact minute. To be habitually "on time" is a virtue, "to be late" a vice.

Just listen to the customers coming into the store. The damned thing stopped, and they still wear it on their wrist as if afraid they'll be naked without it. And how sad they are when they have to take it off and hand it to you. Like bringing someone you love to the hospital and being told you have to leave them there for a while. Their eyes follow the watch as it is being hung on a peg. You'd think the board with pegs and lots of other watches hanging there is a bed-filled hospital ward, and their watch is being left there to linger, perhaps to die in one of the beds.

Speaking of attachment, just listen to some of them speaking of their grandfather clocks. Once in a while, the old clock stops— plain, old dust and grime. It stops, and you'd think it was not the grandfather clock that died but Grandpa himself. And would I, please, could I please, fix it, because without that chime, the house is just not the same. And the old widows and widowers who live alone, and having to move to some smaller quarters, one of the last thing they'd part with would be the old clock. Again that tick-tock. A common pulse, you can say. A pulse that never speeds or slows down, a sign of permanence and tranquility. It becomes the only sound that fills the silence left behind when their spouses are gone.

And one day, when the ticking stops, and the silence becomes terrifying, those oldsters come into the store, schlepping that clock. "Just make it tick, Mr. Klein. Never mind how accurate, just make it tick and, please, make it chime," they tell you with a quivering voice. "Make it tick," they plead, and you'd think they were speaking of their own heartbeat and the fear that if the clock stops, so will their hearts. "And could you fix it as soon as possible?" Or take those newfangled battery-driven watches. The customer comes in and waits while I replace the battery—and presto, the numbers flash again. "A heart transplant," one of the customers said, looking at the watch as he rubbed the front of his chest.

Now the repairing is a whole different matter. You open the thing, and suddenly you're plunged into a whole new world reduced to cogwheels, spindles, springs, some hair-thin, tiny pieces of jewels, and all this has to be viewed with a magnifying glass like looking at a different world through a peephole. Nowadays, batteries have killed much of the fun.

Oh boy! Two pages about being a watchmaker, and you are there in bed coughing your head off and saying to yourself, "What has all this to do with the two of us being sick, old men?" It'll probably bore you and lull you to sleep. Someday you must tell me what you do for a living, or did, as the case may be.

Time to turn on the news—only bad these days, and not even worth watching. But what else is there worth watching? Look at those windows of mine. All frozen over. Ice flowers have formed around the edges, and the shrubs under my window, all white-topped they are like frosting on a cake.

Keep warm and get well soon.

Nathan

P.S. Thanks for the letter opener. It's too beautiful to use it just for opening letters. I keep fingering it the way Muslims rub their amber beads. A great outlet for restless fingers.

CHAPTER
19

It's a mishap day, and all seems to go wrong. I got up on the wrong foot. Literally the wrong one—that is, the left, the one still struggling to bear my full weight. Losing my balance, I reached for the edge of the chair, it toppled, my head went against the table, and here I am on a gurney in what they call the clinic. A bright, overhead surgical spotlight shining straight into my eyes while a middle-aged man dressed in a green surgical gown on top of blue jeans is putting stitches through a gash on the side of my forehead, all the while humming some ditty under his nose.

Miss Hedberg comes into the treatment room. "And what have you done to yourself now?" she exclaims from the door. I turn my head at the sound of her voice, only to be yelled at by the man holding a curved, threaded needle in front of my eye.

"Hey, mister, would you please hold your head still?"

She remains there, the guardian of my health, critically eyeing the surgeon until he is finished.

While still reclining on the operating table, I gaze at the multiple mirrors surrounding the spotlights. Like clones, a full array of old men stare back at me. Sallow faced, loose-jowled, in need of a shave, a white bandage around their heads like those headbands tennis players wear, only broader—this morning, I should have definitely stayed in bed.

During the morning workout, Miss Hedberg is reduced to monosyllabic grunts. The ordeal finished, I spot a collection of canes in the corner.

"Miss Hedberg, do you think I could try one of these?" I nod at that vast assortment, the likes of which I haven't seen since my trip to Mexico and the visit to the shrine of the Lady of Guadeloupe.

"And what is it you will try to do now, Mr. Klein? Break a leg?" she retorts angrily.

Why do I always feel guilty whenever yelled at? Guilty until proved innocent. It's the story of my life, ever since I can remember. Mama would raise her voice at one of my brothers, and before I knew what it was all about, I felt guilty. During a lull in the store, Papa would step out to sit on the stoop and contemplate the cracked sidewalk. He would sit there sullen looking, and I would feel guilty as if I had done something to make him unhappy. I was quite grown-up when I learned that guilt was a family trait, Papa being the guilt-maker, and we, the children and Mama, the recipients.

Late in the afternoon, the bandage compressing my head like a vise, Miss Hedberg, still in a choleric mood, delivers his letter.

Thursday, the 6th of January
Dear Friend,

I chuckled reading your letter about the importance of timepieces. Before they took me into surgery, they removed my wristwatch and ring—one of these days, I must ask them why they do it. I vaguely remember waking up from anesthesia, not knowing where I was, not even knowing my name. It was only later, back in bed, still lost in that postoperative mist of unreality that I felt something missing, as if part of me had been taken away, unaware of what it was until they brought back my watch, and I put it on my wrist. I clearly remember putting it to my ear to listen to it tick, reaching for my glasses to see the time, though a clock was right there on the wall.

They let me sit at my bedside. In fact, they insist on it, and so I sit dressed in that little hospital shirt, open in the back, a string holding it together somewhere in the back of my neck. Size, just about to fit a ten-year-old, the gown hardly reaching to my knees. Paper shoes. Why do they always bring me two? Can't they see I need only one? So I sit there, one leg down, the other only a shiny stump. I wish they would let me wear the prosthesis. Or a sock over it. I feel so naked. Uncovered and on display, it always reminds me of the beggars sitting on the steps leading to the entrance of a church, a naked stump and near it the hat for receiving alms.

This is as good a time as any to sit in my bedside chair and write.

So you looked into the box and thought I was a woodcarver. Not quite, though I used every opportunity I had to carve something. Every time I had a fine piece of wood in front of me, my palms began to itch, eager to give it some shape. I'm a violin maker, and in my workshop, there was always wood, kiln-dried, fragrant, just begging to be shaped. It has been a long time since I made any violins from scratch, so to speak. I spent most of my life repairing them, and not only fiddles, any string instrument, though I love the violin above all the others.

I did well in America. Unlike so many other immigrants, I found employment, you could say, the day I stepped off the boat. God bless New York. There is little one cannot find here if you only know where to look for it. But try to find a fiddle maker—a good one—not a chance. Back in Germany, I had an excellent teacher. Klaubart was his name. The man studied with an old master in Munich who, before that, studied in Italy with another master—the legend goes all the way to the old school of fiddle makers in Cremona and to such luminaries as Stradivarius and Amati. Probably just a fable. But that man understood instruments. God yes! The whole array, from the base fiddle to the cello, to the viola and the violin.

One day, I visited the old man in Munich. He was a hunchback with his chin down on his chest and hardly enough room to wedge in the fiddle. And the man had that unerring ear as he tested the resonance by softly knocking on the surface of every inch of the instrument. Or by softly drawing the bow across the strings, he would know what had gone wrong with the instrument and where it needed improvement. I watched him work, and my heart stopped at the sight of the man taking hold of one of his razor-sharp tools. His hands shook, and yet the moment he touched the violin—steady as they come. With a single, deft motion, he had the tone board off to reveal the innards of the instrument. He worked with the dexterity and swiftness of a surgeon, though I must admit, I never did see a surgeon at work. The few occasions when I was on the table, I was sound asleep.

I don't suppose you play the fiddle. I do, and I must admit that I'm more fond of the instrument as a thing in itself than the music. The mere touching it gives me a thrill. There is gracefulness in the way the back and front curve, in the contour of the waistline and the sinuous configuration of the sound holes. The slenderness of the neck, it has—forgive me the comparison—it has almost a sexual kind of allure. In my eyes, the violin is definitely female. You stroke it, you caress it with your fingers, and it sings. It is subject to changing moods, melancholy and soft at one time, capricious and shrill at others. It can pout like a child and smile with that knowing smile of a mature woman. It can also complain like an abused and neglected woman. You should see how some musicians mistreat their instruments. Shameful.

You see, I firmly believe that each instrument has a unique personality. I would even say a soul of its own. How that comes about is one of those mysteries I was never able to fathom. The wood, the glue, the shape, the way its makers handle all the parts that go into making it—until it becomes a unique creation. And it can wither from neglect. Like we human beings do. When I first arrived in America, I came across a children's book called Pinocchio. A silly little tale, but far from silly to me. Little Pinocchio was a puppet made of wood. At least in the beginning, but then it became endowed with a soul. A real-to-goodness soul, as they say. The same soul that the instrument maker bestows on his creation. The venerable Amati and Geppetto, the puppet maker—a silly comparison, isn't it?

Ah, my friend, I get carried away at the mere thinking of holding an instrument in my hands, touching the neck, touching the pegs. Speaking of peg boxes and pegs, how much artistry has gone into the making of many good instruments?

You should have seen me at my bench after I had finished with a violin, the instrument varnished, dried, ready to put to my chin. The anticipation and then the first notes. Like the first cry of a newborn. The awakening of life. Pure ecstasy. You really have to hear that first sound. Each time, I felt like I had created a new life. And the seeds of my creation are a maple tree, and not just any maple. A special kind it has to be, or a sycamore, or a white pine, the trees hailing *from special places, and the ebony and the rosewoods. And the drying and varnishing. How few musicians really know what goes into the making of an instrument. At best, they only see the exterior, the shape, the color, the wood grain, but there is a structural inside, you may say, the vital organs of the fiddle, the hidden part, the soul. And in the way human beings differ from one another, there are no two fiddles alike. In some instances, the differences are so subtle that it takes an exceptional ear to tell them apart.*

Call me sentimental, if you wish, a mawkish old man, but you see, Nathan, I never married, and the violin was to me the recipient of the many things other men lavish upon other human beings— wife, children, whatever.

And so there you are, my friend. We are even now. You rhapsodized over your watches and clocks, and I took the liberty to fondle a violin, if only in my mind's eyes while sitting here and waiting for the nurse to come and take, what they call, the vital signs. I don't need her. I know I'm getting better. No chills, no fever, I can eat now without that terrible aversion to food I had since surgery.

Yours,
Gerhard

P.S. You wanted to know how I felt about Jerusalem. Well, brace yourself. You're in for an ordeal. The last time I tried to tell my friends about it, they yawned and wanted to know if I found some nice bargains in that smelly bazaar, the Soukh. They had been there, and one wife was looking for a Bedouin dress to use the embroidered part for a pillowcase, but the prices were wicked, she said. And in the first place, she didn't like the way the Arabs looked at her.

Gerhard's next two letters arrive in quick succession, each a bulging envelope.

Wednesday, the 7th of January
Dear Friend,

How boring this place. The food—I have eaten better food in the automat at the Grand Central Station. The other patient in my room died. I don't know when it happened. I woke up in the morning to that silly Glockenspiel they have here to announce that it's time to rise and shine. The other bed was empty, the mattress was bare. I slept right through his demise and the commotion of removing him. I'm getting to be an old man, Nathan. Gone are the days when the least noise would wake me.

Good news though. The doctor, the young man I wrote about, came by. He must be an important man; an entire entourage follows him like so many youngsters, all dressed in white, all listening to him with rapt attention. You would think they are receiving communion, and the man is a high priest, occasionally throwing at them a word or two of wisdom like a benediction. And while he looked at my leg, then at the stitches, a young woman, an intern or a resident, while flipping the pages of my thick chart, recited this long story of *my illness, most of which I couldn't understand, except words like diabetes, bypass, blood pressure. I caught the words blood loss and shock. I never knew that all this happened to me, and by the time they finished, I wished they had gone to some other place to recite that perilous journey of mine from the dying back to the living.*

"How would you like to go home, Gerhard?" the young doctor asked me. I was elated at the sound of the word home even though I knew home meant back here. I was also pleased not to be called Pops.

"When, Doctor?" I made no attempt to conceal my joy.

"A couple of days or so." He smiled. "There is a thing or two we would like to check before we let you go."

And so I'm back to sitting at the bedside writing. Mercifully, the nurse brought me a woolen stocking to fit over the amputated part of my leg.

I'm not much of a writer, but a long time ago, shortly after my arrival in America, I tried to write down some of my thoughts. There was a lot of loneliness during those first few months in the United States. My uncle who lived here either didn't know about my ill-fated attempt of wanting to be a witness, or if he knew, he never brought up the subject. His life revolved around his secondhand bookstore, most of it German literature, the place scattered with folios and other items covered by thick layers of dust and grime.

He was a secretive man, withdrawn, surly, wrapped entirely in his old secondhand books. Can you imagine—the man never asked me what happened during the war. He was here, and to him, the war took place over there in Europe, and that was that. To live with him, I may as well have joined the order of monks sworn to silence. It may sound strange to you, but in those days, I had no one to write to or to write for. My letters home remained unanswered. I had made a few friends, but here in America, the wounds of the war were still raw. The Germans were still branded with the same iron. "Nazis, the whole lot of them." To just sit there in my room and write was akin to making fiddles, knowing that no one would ever play them, or you repairing watches no one would ever wear. I decided to move out, and while packing my belongings, I simply tore up all those scribbled notes and threw them away. But now I have you to write to.

You wanted to know about Jerusalem. A strange place, the hospital, for writing about Jerusalem while sitting in my short hospital gown, a blanket throw over my shoulders, biding my time, waiting to get well, wondering if I ever will, hoping that someday I will walk out of here on my one good leg. I visited that city only once but revisited it in my mind over and over again, each time recalling another detail, insignificant at the time in the light of so many other overpowering emotions, but coming back and back like the clearing of a morning mist, allowing me to see things obscured until then.

I arrived there shortly after the war of 1967. I was an American citizen then, single and free to come and go as I wished. Jerusalem. A flash of light. An illumination. How does one write that single word without closing one's eyes for one brief moment and seeing it all over again? I don't know what the sight of that city does to Jewish people when they experience it for the first time. To me, brought up as a Christian with all the sanctification of the cross, its glorification and sacredness, the Mount of Olives, the Via Dolorosa, the Golgotha, the martyrdom of the Lord, the city with its hills, seemed less of a dwelling place and more like a holy shrine.

I walked up and down the streets and had a feeling that it was here where it all began. Jerusalem was the essence of everything that ever happened, the rest of human history only an epilogue. All those Sunday morning sermons held by the old pastor seemed only myths, parables, and legends, while here was reality. Palpable, visible, and audible. Here I was, surrounded by a throng of commuters, other tourists, local populace, taxi drivers, the cars honking with a fury, the church spires and the glistening dome in the distance, an ice-cream vendor surrounded by a bevy of chirping youngsters. The holy and the profane side by side.

But I'm ahead of myself. It started at the airport the minute we landed. The door opened, and I was struck by the sound of singing and loud hand-clapping. Down on the tarmac stood a group of newly arrived youngsters, perhaps fifty, their bundles at their feet, sleep still in their eyes, their clothes disheveled, looking bewildered and unsure of themselves. The clapping and singing was done by other young people, better dressed, presumably their hosts.

Long before the airport limousine came to a stop, I caught a glimpse of the city, and it struck my eyes like a mirage, unreal, almost unbelievable. I stepped down, my feet touching the ground, a ground *unlike any other I had stepped on before. A strange current seemed to emanate from the plaza stones and flow through my entire being. I wanted to tiptoe, to walk in silence, as if the sound created by my thick-soled tourist shoes would profane the ground.*

I was only half-aware of the people around me. Elegant women with their shopping bags, youngsters on their way to or from school, the sidewalk belonging to them and their playful ambling, two young men dressed in black gabardines, black hats riding low on the back of their heads, earlocks dangling with each step, walking and gesticulating, seemingly oblivious to the world, to anything but their discussion at hand. Two soldiers walked by, caps stashed underneath the epaulets, embroidered yarmulkes covering the top of their heads, their bearing soldierly with that air of confidence of the young daring the whole world.

An old man stood at the corner, waiting to cross the street. He was dressed in a black gabardine coat, his long beard silvery, my image of an old prophet. Our eyes met, and he was gazing at me with eyes that seemed to be appraising and challenging. He stood tall with none of that stoop of the frightened men in the ghetto, the ones I saw on so many previous occasions. For one brief moment, I wondered if the man gazed at me with a look of recognition. But then, ever since I had stepped off the airplane, I had the disquieting sensation that all the men and women, young and old, were staring at me in recognition of who I once was, and I saw contempt in their eyes and reproach for the part I played a long time ago.

Suddenly I felt as an intruder. That I had no right being here. I had traveled abroad before, but at no time did I feel so much the unwanted, the man who had come to visit the scene of his crime, you could say. I know, it was my own delusion, for the people were polite, in many ways more cordial than those on the street of Manhattan, and yet I couldn't rid myself of it, and it lingered on for the entire time I was there.

I shouldn't be telling you this, but there was one occasion when my eyes inadvertently fell on the rolled-up sleeve of a middle-aged man. The shirt he wore had some geometrical crisscross pattern, and for a moment it looked like that damned armband with the Jewish star on his sleeve. I broke out in a cold sweat and quickly averted my eyes. Further down the street, I saw a municipal building. I don't remember now what it was, but there, high on a pole fluttering in the breeze, was the flag with the star of David surrounded by blue stripes. I looked at it for a long time. Strange, this time-warp association of mine between the armband, that past symbol of debasement and now the national emblem of a people. One seemed to cancel the other. But still it was there in the back of my mind as a prickly reminder who I was and who they were.

What is there to say about the Yad Vashem that words will not diminish? The senses take it in, but only a fraction of it. I cannot conceive of any human being absorbing it in its entirety. Like a deluge of the senses, it threatens to inundate you, and you must avert your eyes, if only for a brief moment, like a man drowning and in need to raise his head above waters for a breath of air. And no amount of words could describe it, for no words have been invented yet to describe what that sanctuary depicts. The music, and the voices come at you from the throats of those walking to their doom. Soft, yet penetrating every fiber like a dirge accompanied by a mournful drumbeat, louder than any drumbeat I had ever heard.

Looking at the murals, my eyes kept shifting from pictures of the many walking to their doom to those helmeted guards, the men who perpetrated such unbelievable horror. Without wanting to, I would find myself staring into the eyes of those men with machine guns, and they were looking straight at me from below the rim of their steel helmets. Eyes without the least trace of pity, eyes with chilling stares of the lustful murderer. And those eyes kept telling me, "You were one of us, remember?"

And so I kept walking through the exhibit, only part of me conscious of my surroundings, like walking in a delirium, feverish at one moment, chilled with horror of what I saw the next. My legs trembled, my heart beat against my ribcage as if my chest had become too small for it, and I had to hold on to a railing. There were moments when I wanted to get out of there, run, never look at it again. Better yet, run into the arms of someone who would embrace me and tell me that all that I saw there never happened, that it was only a nightmare.

I walked on and wept. Others wept too. That's about all I could do, weep and let the tears run down my face without wiping them.

And so I went on in that slow, shuffling gait, along with the many visitors, looking, not wanting to see and yet compelled to see. And all the while, all of me kept saying no, not we, not the men and the women I grew up with, loved at one time, honored and esteemed, they couldn't have done that, and at the same time knowing that they did. We did. Oh yes, we did. This and so much more.

Many wept, but none wept the way I did. Mine was a compound weeping. Sorrow, infamy, disgrace, a thousand crushing emotions. Above all, guilt. For what was done to the millions. For what we did. For what I did. And there was shame, shame for the silence of all those countrymen of mine who pretended not have seen it while it was being perpetrated, and continued with their silence after the war was over.

Strange as it may sound, it was here, more so than ever before, that the enormity of the events struck me. And mind you, I was there in Kostowa when it happened, well not exactly at the time, two days later, but the footprints of that carnage were still visible on the sidewalks, the alleys, and the back of those dilapidated houses.

Forgive me, my friend, for writing all this. No doubt it must be painful for you to read. You, at least, have someone to share with all those troubling visions. I have no one. Early on, I tried—only impassive and cold faces. Enough, enough, those faces were telling me. The war was over, and the sooner forgotten the better for all of us. But I couldn't forget. And so I gave up speaking about it and plunged into a kind of suffocating silence. And now I saw you, and it was you who brought up the subject of the Yad Vashem, and so I took the liberty to unburden myself. For there is nothing so crushing as a pain one cannot share.

Strange, isn't it, that I, Gerhard Reichenberg, should have had to seek all these years for someone to listen, then finding him, and it's you, one of those many whose faces are depicted on those walls. And to you I present my pain. What venomous offering it must be to you.

Yad Vashem came to an end, and the door opened to that brilliant Jerusalem light. With my eyes still clouded by what I saw, I stepped outside and went on my pilgrimage. For that is what it was—a pilgrimage. Others may have gone up the steep Via Dolorosa—Yad Vashem was mine. Not in search of faith but of forgiveness. I kept on walking, without any particular destination, just to walk and look at the people—proud, carefree, dignified, a medley of the Nordic blond and the dark-haired, olive skin, dark eyes—the Middle East.

I walked into a post office to buy stamps. A short queue, and I took my place in the back of the line. The woman at the counter, and the one who just approached it, both gray-haired and well past middle age, greeted each other with a broad-grinned "Shalom" and immediately switched to speaking to one another in flawless German with an unmistaken Berlin accent. Old acquaintances, it seemed. Berlin in Jerusalem. What must they have seen, what must they have lived through before coming here, the one selling stamps, the other wanting to know how her daughter Miriam was coming along. In parting, the stamp buyer said, "Auf wiedersehen," and the other smilingly replied, "Shalom."

My turn came, and I said shalom in the way I would have said buon giorno *on entering an establishment anywhere in Italy, but the older woman behind the counter raised her eyes and replied, "Guten tag," in the same perfect German. Even my shalom failed to conceal who I was. She seemed neither surprised nor offended by my reply in German. She must have thought that I was an Israeli of German origin, one of many in this city.*

I walked on—boutiques, a tobacco shop with postcards and tourist memorabilia on display, a butcher, a baker—life mundane, blasphemous to my eye still riveted to the tales of the patriarchs and the paths trodden by Jesus and the apostles. But there was a quickening in the air, vibrant and animating. Jerusalem was in a hurry. Only a few walked slowly with the lumbering gait of tourists with cameras dangling from their necks.

I went to the Wall. Another sight to overwhelm the senses, this one by its—well, how shall I describe it—almost otherworldliness. Hundreds of men, and men only. They prayed in a hurry and with a fervor I had never seen anyone pray before. Not my fellow Christian, not the few Muslims whom I saw prostate themselves on a prayer rug in a mosque. But most striking was the intensity of their prayer, a kind that seemed to be coming right from their innermost. And hurried too, as if the channels through which their prayers were to reach the Almighty were about to be closed any moment. We

Christians get down on our knees, piously fold our hands, bend our heads in surrender, and most of the time only murmur the prayers, and when we sing, it is in a tinny voice of supplication. But not these men at the Wall. They shook, they bent back and forth, twisted their torsos, waved their arms, pulled their beards and those earlocks, and they sang. God Almighty, did they ever sing.

I stood at the wall bewildered, mesmerized by the sight of so many praying, right there in the open, the sky the roof, no stained-glass windows, no building with spires in the shape of hands held up in supplication, no organs playing softly, no aroma of incense wafting through the air, only an ancient wall, undecorated, the stones roughly hewn, tufts of weed growing in the cracks.

An old man tapped my shoulder, handed me a yarmulke, and speaking Yiddish asked me if I would like to don—he pointed at the prayer shawl draped around his shoulders—and seeing me shake my head, he pointed at a stack of prayer books on a fold-up table a little ways from us. I refused again, and he looked at me reproachfully. He said something that sounded like, "You're a Jew, no?" and before I had a chance to reply, two other men approached and drew his attention. They looked like tourists in well-cut double-breasted suits, white shirts, and neckties, one with a small camera bulging his pocket. The old man went through the same motions, the table with books, the yarmulke, and a stalk of prayer shawls.

I walked away to resume my quiet contemplation of the men,

their eyes shut, their heads shaking in that strange ritualistic kind of praying I had never seen.

Ah, yes. Years later, there was a time when I too prayed and prayed that hard. With all my body and soul, as they say. I was told that I may lose my leg. Wounds had formed around my ankle and along the top of my foot, and they were afraid that gangrene may set in. I suppose a sinner doesn't bend God's ear. As you see, I lost my leg.

You must forgive me for stopping here. I wish I could go on writing about Jerusalem. My hand seems to have gathered a momentum of its own and doesn't wish to stop. Like a child with a new toy, I would like to go on writing, transported now on memories, some beautiful, some bittersweet. But daylight is nearly over, and I must return to bed. Even with the head raised, writing is difficult, and the light too dim for my defective eyes. Damned diabetes.

Thursday, the 8th of January
Dear Nathan,

What a frustrating day. Morning rounds, and the nurse arrived, trailing behind her an orderly pushing a gurney. To my question where I'm being taken, she looked perplexed.

"Didn't your doctor tell you that you'll be presented at Surgical Grand Rounds this morning?"

"You mean, I have to be there?"

"Oh, they got quite a few cases this morning. It'll be just a few minutes."

Before I could object, the orderly moved the gurney against my bed, and I was helped onto it and wheeled to the amphitheater. Some ordeal, this being there near the lectern, surrounded by projectors, x-ray viewing boxes, a young woman in a white uniform with a stethoscope around her neck reading from a chart, and all those in the amphitheater looking down at me. My name was "This seventy-two-year-old white male entered the hospital ..." After that, things became too complicated, especially as the lights dimmed and an entire panel of x-rays was shown.

It was demeaning. I suppose there must be some who may enjoy being the centerpiece of attention even for the ten or fifteen minutes that it lasted. I for one felt that I was being placed in a store window, all the pedestrians on the sidewalk stopping and gaping. In time, my solo entrance on the stage was over—no good mornings, no good-byes, no thank you, no applause.

But let this "seventy-two-year-old white male" continue with where I left off yesterday.

Gerhard must have been interrupted or ran out of paper, for the next few pages were unadorned and written with a different pen. For a moment, I was taken aback by the handwriting, as if it weren't his own. The slant was different, and some of the letters were more ornate and outright frilly. But it was Gerhard all right with his customary flourish.

Dear Nathan,

Back to Jerusalem. The next day while sauntering through the "New City," as against the "Old Jerusalem," I passed a music store. I never could walk by a music store without stopping and letting my eyes feast over the instruments displayed in the window. A. M. Schneider and Sons, said the sign in English and Hebrew. So many Schneiders, Schusters, and Tischlers here. I once knew a Schneider, a tall, skinny, young man, Albert was his name. An apprentice in the same violin repair shop. There were four of us, all in our teens. Albert, a prankster, was the thorn in the side of the foreman, dexterous though with his hands. The chisel and reamers would spring to life the moment Albert touched them.

We were friends attracted to each other by our diametrical opposites in temperaments. I was the plodder, heavy-handed but dedicated to what I was doing at the time, even if took hours, while Albert was impatient, flighty, and with a flair for innovation. Albert left one day, and for a while no one spoke of it, as if he had never been one of us. A strange silence, a make-believe-nothing-is-happening kind. A lot of our Jewish coworkers, colleagues in the shop, occupants of the apartment down on the floor below us, would simply leave while we pretended not to have noticed it, as if sworn to some sinister silence on such matters.

A.M. Schneider and Son. I stepped back from the window and looked at the sign again. The letter A could stand for Aaron, Abraham, Arthur. What strange coincidence it would be if the man here in Jerusalem, thirty years later, would be Albert, the same fellow apprentice of half a century ago. I entered the store to the sound of a chime. A young man, lean and swarthy, wearing an embroidered yarmulke attached to his curly hair by two hairpins, stood behind the counter. Leaning forward, he spoke insistently to the customers there, a young woman, a heavyset man, and a boy, perhaps eight years old, apparently their son. Not wishing to interrupt, I walked over to a display of ornately carved wooden music stands. They spoke Hebrew, and I couldn't even get the gist of what they were saying except for an occasional "okay," a phrase that seemed to have caught on all over the world. At one point, the boy picked up one of the violins, put it under his chin, and drew the bow across, producing a scratchy sound. The boy looked apologetically at his parents, at the man behind the counter, then threw a quick glance at me and put the violin down.

The young man behind the counter shifted his attention to me and looked at me questioningly.

"May I speak to Mr. Schneider?" I addressed him in English.

"My name is Schneider, and what can I do for you?" He spoke with a clipped British accent.

"I once knew a man, his name was Albert Schneider, but that was a long time ago, and I wondered if he was the owner of this shop."

"Albert is my father's name, and may I know, sir, what is the nature of your inquiry?"

"Sir," he addressed me. An officious kind of sir that carried just *a tinge of animosity and suspicion. His smile vanished. And again I was gripped by the same edge of misgiving of having come here. He kept looking at me the way others did on the street, some in the queue on entering the Yad Vashem, even the man, the woman, and their young son whose attention shifted from the violins to me. Once again, I felt the same remorse of having trespassed, having no right to be here.*

"My name is Reichenberg. I'm a visitor and saw the sign Schneider and just wondered if by some chance Mr. A. Schneider—"

"Just one moment, sir." He didn't let me finish. Instead, he opened a door leading to a room in the back of the counter and spoke to someone in there in rapid Hebrew. "Aba," he addressed the man inside. Aba—father, this much I understood, and he called my name. Through the partly open door, I could see a workbench brightly lit by an array of overhead lamps.

It was Albert. I knew it the moment he entered still wiping his hands on his apron. It must have been thirty years since I saw him the last time. Somewhat paunchy, he was no longer the skinny lad of years ago. He had grown a well-trimmed, speckled, gray beard. His once luxurious brown hair had become sparse and silky. He wore a yarmulke way in the back of his head. A double chin, flabby jowls, his once oval face was now angular. He wore a blue apron, stained, the edges frayed. Dear God, I could have sworn it was the same apron we wore when we were youngsters. Carefree at day's end, we used those aprons to playfully swat one another across the rear and give chase through the empty workshop, and yes, I suddenly remembered, we used old and discarded bows in mock sword fights.

He came out and stood behind the counter right next to his son. He stared at me with squinting eyes and a deep frown. I wasn't sure if it was the brightly lit showroom or if Albert was looking at me with his eyes narrowed like those of a man trying recall things past, images long forgotten, or were they eyes of a man seething with anger? He left the counter and slowly came forward to where I stood, halting a few feet in front of me. And so we stood facing each other silently. I wanted to approach him, to shake hands with him, but looking at his pensive gaze, I lost courage and stood there tongue-tied. I have often wondered what Albert thought at that moment, but as I kept watching him, his eyes suddenly grew large and penetrating. He raised his arm, slowly at first, as if undecided whether to shake hands with me, but his hand continued to go up, and for one brief moment, I was sure he was going to slap my face. I stood still. His hand ceased going up, and with his index finger, he pointed at the door behind me and shouted, "Raus!"

It was a loud shout that seemed to penetrate every nook in the now quiet showroom. It must have jarred his son, the customers, as much as it jarred me. I stood there riveted to the spot as if suddenly having received a blow to my head and as yet unable to fully comprehend what was happening. Albert let his hand fall down to his side, and I saw him swallow hard, his Adam's apple bobbing up and down, the corners of his mouth drooping with anger. Or was it *sorrow? He must have seen me hesitate. He took one step forward and, raising his hand again, shouted once more, "Raus!" though this time his voice was less shrill.*

I opened the door. The chime rang once more, though it no longer carried that pleasing dulcet sound. I stood on the sidewalk, undecided where to go from there. It mattered little in the bustling commercial center, and I just walked on, no longer looking at the faces of the many pedestrians. I was unwanted here, and it took Albert, that old friend of mine, to say it clearly, to say it crudely perhaps, but at last divested of all the silent innuendoes and subterfuge of those around me.

I had been thrown out of his store convinced that he knew nothing of what I did during the war. His was a summary judgment of guilty for all of us, and a summary dismissal. Raus!—out with you.

It rankled, God yes, it rankled and shamed me to have been thrown out of a man's store, the man an old friend of mine. Thrown out in the presence of his son and a family of three. Censured, made feel to be utterly worthless and despicable. It was a "Raus!" more than the casual word to leave. It carried the derisive meaning in the way we would say, "Beat it, out with you, get lost!" Was it simply a manner of speech or was this "raus" of his a distant echo of one or of many such "Raus!" shouted at him by my countrymen as they threw him out?

And yet, after the initial wave of outrage had passed, and as I went on sauntering up and down the streets, I felt overtaken by a strange calm. I was shown the door; I was shown how unwanted I was here. I was chastised. For the first time since I stepped on the soil of this city.

I was being castigated for things others had done, for things I did. Not much of a punishment considering the enormity of those deeds, a verbal slap in the face only, but a punishment just the same. In this, and in the walk through the Yad Vashem, I began to understand the sinners through the ages, the many who walked the Via Dolorosa, some on their knees by way of a self-inflicted punishment. I used to scoff at all that piety, at the hour-long kneeling, the walking on one's knees toward the altar, the fasting and other forms of self-flagellation for sins committed, real or imagined. I no longer scoffed. It suddenly became clear in an uplifting sort of way. Gerhard Reichenberg, the penitent in Jerusalem. My first penitence for my past deeds.

It was the "Raus!" and the outstretched hand of my old friend Albert showing me the door, mingled with the images at the Yad Vashem, that accompanied me into my seat in the airplane on my way back home. I had to change planes in Frankfurt, that old hometown of mine. During the four hours of waiting for my flight to New York, I sat at the designated gate. Not once did I venture into the main terminal and its upper deck with its cocktail lounges and restaurants. I had lost all desire to even cast a glance at the city skyline in the far-off distance. I couldn't. I felt sick to my stomach even at the thought of seeing it. Nor did I pick up the many telephones on *the wall to call relatives, old friends, old neighbors. And just as I felt a sense of alienation and nonbelonging on my arrival in Jerusalem, I felt even more so here in the city where I was born, and toward the familiar faces of those I once lovingly called family.*

The plane taxied for takeoff, gathered speed with that exhilarating sensation of flight, and I still saw Jerusalem. Etched in my mind, I kept seeing it with my eyes open or closed. The dome, the men at prayer, the young soldiers, the flag hoisted on top of the tall building, that once-upon-a-time badge of denigration now becoming the symbol of pride and power. But above all, it was the Yad Vashem, a wound deep and painful. And those men in black gabardine, once cowering Jews in the ghetto, men who walked alongside crumbling adobe walls, furtively, effacingly, trying to become invisible, for being visible was tantamount to perishing. Here in the city, they walked with a proprietary stride. Here they belonged; they always have and always will, they seemed to say. The old man at the intersection stood patiently while waiting for the traffic to slow down enough for him and a few other pedestrians to cross, and when the time was right, he stepped off the curb and walked, daring with his eyes the oncoming cars. I wouldn't have dared to do this in downtown Manhattan, and the traffic was just as bad.

I can see you reading my description of this city of saints, the ancient and latter-day kind, and shaking your head in wonderment at all this elation, all this piety and saintliness. No, Nathan, I'm not a pious man, not as pious as my mother and one or two of my aunts. I only tell you this to describe my state of mind at the time.

You have been there, and I'm curious to know how you felt. But all in good time.

I'm chomping at the bits to be discharged from here and get back to my old room, to Miss Hedberg, and God willing to catch a glimpse of you. Will they ever let me go back?

Yours,
Gerhard

CHAPTER
20

Two weeks have gone by, and there is no letter. I'm perplexed and troubled. By now, I have seen enough illness and its unpredictable outcome to suspect the worst. Staring through the window at the gray wintry sky and the banks of soot-crusted mounds of snow, my mind drifts into the realm of gloom. I see him dead, I see him alive his other leg gone too, and he looks like a broken mannequin, crushed, withdrawn, not wanting to speak to anyone. Miss Hedberg, sensing my concern, and quite likely having similar forebodings, arrives for my morning exercises, and as soon as she gets through the door with the wheelchair, she shrugs and raises her hands. To my inquiry about his health, she can only tell me that the nurse on Gerhard's floor looked into the chart, read the doctor's notes, and found no reason why he was still being kept there.

I wrote to him twice but received no answer. I telephoned, and the call was intercepted at the nurse's desk.

"Mr. Reichenberg, did you say? Now let me see. We have a Reichen, something or Eichen something … Yeah, I got it right here. He is in room number 24 A, listed as condition fair."

To all my other inquiries about him, I was told, "Sorry, sir, we cannot give out such info on the phone, but if you wish to visit him, visiting hours are from …"

I didn't bother to listen to her nasal and bored monotone, a perfect copy of a prerecorded telephone message.

It is the next day, late in the afternoon. Miss Hedberg bursts into the room, her face radiating joy. "He's here!" she shouts from the door. "He's here, Mr. Klein, and wait till you see him. He gained weight, his cheeks are pink, he is ten years younger since he left here."

"Can I see him?"

"Not yet, Mr. Klein. Let's not rush things. He's back but not quite well."

"Did he say anything?"

"I'm in a rush to catch the bus into town, Mr. Klein, and didn't have the time to speak to him."

"The box." I nod at the thing he left with me for safekeeping.

"Sure, just keep it till tomorrow—but I must go now." And she leaves as suddenly as she arrived.

With a sense of relief, as if having found a thing I thought irretrievably lost, I turn on the light using my left hand, not realizing I have done so until I hear the click.

Friday, the 3rd of February
Dear Gerhard,

And so you're back. I would like to crow, "Didn't I tell you?" But that would be a lie. To tell the truth, I was worried. More than you think. These last few years, so many friends of mine have left the scene, cashed in their chips, as the saying goes, and my mind, morbid to start with, went wild conjuring up all kinds of disasters.

Your last letters, all pages combined, make up a whole tome.

Your experiences in Jerusalem were hardly those I would have expected. I must make a confession. In one of your previous letters, you mentioned having gone there. And to be frank, I just couldn't place you there. Somehow you didn't belong there. To me, you are still a man of disguises. There are times when I see you, the man on the bench, the old man with a cane, the limping man … well, I need not elaborate the way you looked on that day when I first recognized you. But then there are the many times when you are still the Herr Arbeitsleiter of so many years ago, the tall man with an arrogant stride and that commanding presence. The man I hated with every fiber. And what is missing to that inner eye of mine is that man in between. And there surely has to be one hiding somewhere. None of us is truly all black or all white. We are all shades of gray.

I'm sorry to say, but until I read your long letter, you were still the young Arbeitsleiter walking up and down the streets of Jerusalem, and I kept saying to myself, What in hell is he doing there and why did he go there in the first place? So much for the vagaries of my mind. But you see, that Arbeitsleiter is hard to erase. He is drawn with the kind of ink I'm having trouble rubbing out. He is still there, and he comes to my mind when I least expect him or want him to be there. But so is the other man, the Gerhard, "the sweet old man," by the pronouncement of our mutual admirer Miss Hedberg, the recent Gerhard, the man who can love and weep, the man the artist, the man with a conscience—what the hell, I was never good at flattery.

I was deeply moved as I came across your walk through the Yad Vashem, for I too walked through it and wept. I too saw men familiar, not those wearing helmets, my kind, one of which I recognized, enough to make me avert my gaze and avoid seeing and listening to anything but my own heartbeat hammering at my temples. And so you see, Gerhard, for one brief moment, we both walked together, and as I read on, we wept together, though at different times and perhaps for different reasons, you identifying with the perpetrators, and I with the victims.

A gap remains though. One I'm having trouble bridging, and with each successive letter of yours, each another revelation of who *and what you really are now, I'm less sure of who you were then. And if my ability to gauge people is right, tell me please, how did a man like you become a thug in the first place? And not just a marching, arm-waving kind. You were a true believer of that creed of men and women gone berserk.*

But all in good time. First get well. At least well enough to sit there on the bench and catch that little bit of sunshine that once in a while manages to sneak down through the heavily overcast skies.

Nathan

His next letter arrives promptly.

Saturday, February the 4th
Dear Nathan,

Thank you for the return of my tools. And, of course, your note. What would I ever do without your letters, especially those I received in the hospital? A madhouse that place, I tell you. They minister to your limbs, heart, arteries, and God knows what other parts of your innards in need of fixing, and in this they seem to be the best of their kind. If they could only be half as good in catering to your brain. Reduced to "a white, seventy-two-year-old male with a chief complaint of, etc.," you become a thing, a curiosity to be shared with others, a moon rock on display, if you will. And so I was in that state of limbo—one day well enough to be discharged, the next day, after a sleepless night of anticipation, the nurse arrives and shakes her head—not yet, another test, another jab with a needle in the arm, the test results not right yet, and in need to be repeated the next day, and the same story the day after. Disoriented in time, reduced to a never-varying routine of waking up, eating cold cereal, toiletry, and rounds, one tends to simply drift, tomorrows being a mindless repetition of yesterdays. And so you sit in your chair by the bedside, your head nods, and you become numb and listless, in a kind of state of torpor.

I didn't write. Beyond an ill-defined awareness of existing, I felt nothing. I had nothing to say.

God, it's good to be back again among the living, not just the existing. To look at the dimpled, angelic face of Miss Hedberg, to receive a letter from you, to caress the smooth surface of my toolbox—that palpable sense of identity of who I am, an affirmation that I'm more than that while male in a look-alike hospital gown that barely reaches below my pubis. And raising the blinds on my window, I can see that patch of a garden. Not much to look at as yet, but soon the snow will melt, and my bench will be there once again, a place—an altar to meditate, sometimes even to pray a little.

You wanted to know how I became a Nazi. A hoodlum—your favored word for it—in retrospect, as good a word as any. How often have I asked myself that same question? There were times when I thought I had the answers, and then something happened, and my neatly spun theory went to pieces, and I had to go and search *elsewhere to explain what seemed so inexplicable. Was it in our nature to be those tromp, tromp, marching, singing, arm-waving, Heil Hitler, outstretched-arm, saluting thugs—another one of your favored words? Or was there something in the air we breathed as we grew up, the words we heard at the dinner table, on the streets, on the playground, maybe as far back as in the lullabies our mothers and nanny's sang to us? I just don't know, Nathan. Was it nature or nurture, that age-old quandary. I just don't know.*

Whatever the truth, I have an aversion to inborn traits, especially when it concerns an entire people. Born that way, they say; it's in their blood, the old Huns; once a Barbarian, always a Barbarian; since the dawn of history, they haven't changed one bit—how often have I heard it said in my presence, most of the time the speaker unaware of who I was. Even if there was a kernel of truth in it, I find it repugnant. It smacks so much of that pernicious race theory, that madness of the twentieth century, the very same that caused me so much anguish and cost so many lives. A dangerous road, slippery, and once you fall under its sway, there is no stopping. Superior races—inferior races—God, how many times have I heard it, and how many tears have I shed because of it.

Inborn racial characteristics? No, my friend, it won't hold water. Too simplistic, too pat an answer to a very complex matter of why a people act one way at one time and another way at some other. As to nurture, look at my own family. Nothing unusual there, just an ordinary middle-class family. Not rich but neither poor. Merchant and craftsmen, most of them. City dwellers since anyone could remember.

My father, and I start with him following an old habit of placing our attributes on the shoulders of our fathers. He too went to war. World War One. He went to fight and to die for God and the Kaiser, his two towering authorities. Went with that burning ambition to plunge his bayonet into the belly of some Frenchman or a Russian; he wasn't too choosy. A young man when he left, a cockade in his buttonhole, reeling drunk as he marched off to the train station, my mother told the story of his induction into the ranks. He aged in the trenches. Verdun—a lifetime telescoped into a few months on the Western front. At war's end, he came home, a wound in his leg, painful and foul smelling, a silent man. He refused to speak to anyone except his old cat.

Once he regained enough trust in his fellow man, he told us the story of how they wheeled him into the makeshift surgery barrack to amputate his stinking leg. Just then the door burst open, and someone yelled that the war was over, and they all ran out, including the surgeon still wearing his blood-covered apron. They ran out to listen to the silence. No more cannonade in the distance, just stillness. Whooping it up and getting drunk on the spot, they forgot about him and later on wheeled him into the amputee section, his gangrenous leg wound untouched. They left him there with others who had a leg or an arm removed, most of them either still groggy from anesthesia or raving after discovering what had been done to them. He had a *raging fever and was out of his head for more than a week, but the leg healed, of sorts.*

We were still little when he began telling us stories about the war. Bedside stories they were, fairytales like Hansel and Gretel, and he kept on telling them over and over again. I was a little boy. My sister, Helga, was two years older, and we kept asking him, "Papa, would you tell us again about the time when you kept catching rats and cooking them to have something to eat? Or the time when the parapet of the trench caved in, and you had to dig yourself out with your bare hands, and how about the time when you were naked down to your waist, and a contingent of French soldiers reached your sector, and you had to fight them hand-to-hand using only your bayonet?"

He was a storyteller, my father. He told us those stories and made them sound so heroic, as if this alone was the greatest moment in his life. And then he showed us medals. A piece of felt and all the medals pinned on, shiny as if he had gotten them just the day before, for he kept polishing them every so often while we watched and listened with awe to what he did to receive them. Some, I recall, were his, and some belonged to Grandfather who fought in the Franco-Prussian war.

And of course, there were those pictures, brown and faded most of them, Grandfather in his Kaiser Army uniform, father as a young man in uniform surrounded by his Kameraden, their arms linked, smiling at the camera, one with bandages around his head. Happy, smiling, father even grew a mustache a la Kaiser Willi. Shaved it off after he came home. Strange, this story of the mustache. It all came back so vividly when less than twenty years later men began growing mustaches again. Short ones this time, toothbrush variety, a la Herr Hitler, the new idol to worship. And much later, I was no longer the child. I too contributed to that album. There I was on one of the last pages. Not much of a military figure, no medals, just standing there, smiling sheepishly at the camera, one showing me with my arms around a young woman—no, not Esta—this one blonde, wearing a Dirndl, a Bavarian kind of costume with a Tyrolean hat and feather. Three generations of uniforms. Is there a message in there? I suspect there is, but I'm not sure.

Of course, there was Mama, our Mutti. Strange how in all those pictures she always stood in the back row or behind someone, unimportant, like a prop on the stage just put there to create a mood. A pert little woman, soft spoken, and affectionate. Just looking at the pictures, you would never know that she was a woman with an iron will and unbending principles. It was later, much later when all that madness was over that she slowly approached the front of the stage like a main actor who waited in the wings for the minor ones to finish their lines before making his entry. She was deeply religious with a simplistic kind of an unbending faith in right and wrong, the centerpiece of which was her conviction that there was an all-seeing and forever-watchful God looking into the hearts of men and judging. Not a very forgiving God.

Was it my father who paved the footpath for me to follow? As it may have been his father who paved it for him? Was it Mama with her unbending sense of what was right and what was wrong? I don't know. I wish my sister, Helga, had survived the war. She was the product of the same upbringing, and perhaps she could have given me some of the answers to that forever-vexing riddle.

Enough for now. It's long past Miss Hedberg's visit with the usual knocking on the door, poking her head in, wanting to know how I feel, and asking, "Anything I can do for your, Mr. Reichenberg?" A clear disguise for wanting to know if there is a letter to be delivered.

Your friend,
Gerhard

CHAPTER
21

"Now that's just what I hoped for." The door opens, and Miss Hedberg announces her arrival. "You've become friends. Ja, ja, you no longer look at my face; it's my pocket now, the one that has a letter in it. To you I have become Ulrica Hedberg the postman."

"Miss Lonely Heart," I say, "a better title would be the Matchmaker of Malmö, but didn't you get the gender mixed up a little?"

She blushes and hands me a thick envelope. Chock full of pages, it weighs heavily.

"We've become friends, did you say? Not quite, Miss Hedberg. Just two old men with nothing better to do," I say and hold up the letter like a trophy.

"You wouldn't care to pay someone a visit?" she asks with a note of skepticism.

On the way to the workout, she is in a chatty mood.

"You have a son and his wife to visit you, and she is beautiful. Stunning. And the way she dresses. Some people are lucky. So many here have nobody to visit them. Breaks your heart to see them in a room they share with another resident, one side of the room filled with people—they have to bring in extra chairs—the other end just a single bed and no one there to visit. So many lonely people."

"Are you telling me that Gerhard has no visitors?"

"Well, only once in a great while."

"A visit, Miss Hedberg? You want me to visit him? In a wheelchair?"

"Well, why not?"

We part. Miss Hedberg leaves with her chin held high, sphinxlike, part challenging, part mysterious. Until now, I have given little thought to visiting Gerhard. I cannot see myself looking up at the man from my vintage of sitting in a wheelchair. Perhaps there is even more than the wheelchair. I was crippled. I was crippled once upon a time, a different kind of crippling as I looked into that man's face. A communal kind, diminished, frightened, cowering, the kind of crippling they engendered in all of those they subjugated. No, I will not be seen like that again. Not by the once *Arbeitsleiter*, or by the man who years later walked down the streets of Jerusalem feeling unworthy of being there.

Monday, the 6th of February
Dear Gerhard,

I read your letter. Forgive me for saying so, but your description of your family has been a commonplace portrait of many German families. After the war had ended, after all the tears that had been shed for the many victims, after all the committed indignities and trials, to us who managed to survive that man-made hell, few doors remained open, and all too many of these were equally forbidding, but of this some other time. And so I lived there among you for another four years and had an intimate look at the German people.

In a way, you were right when it comes to lumping people. The Japanese were the bloodthirsty cruel Samurai, the Germans the Huns, those incorrigible barbarians. Both were drawn with the hand of caricature. Pure and simple, they were the enemies and as such had to be lumped together without allowing any exceptions. They had to be reduced to something one could hate without pangs of conscience. Forgive me again for saying it, but in those years of madness, it was Germany who was at the forefront of lumping. They elevated caricature into an art that in time became the centerpiece of their Reich's culture. Especially when it came to Jews, Gypsies, Slavs, and other so-called unsavory human beings.

I just glanced at what I wrote. Bitter words, I know, but today I'm a bitter man. It has to do with my Sunday visitors. My son is a spineless man. And tactless. Margot, my daughter-in-law, insists on wearing a gold necklace with a cross and went on telling me how spiritually uplifting her confession was that morning. And what is most galling is to see my son sitting there and nodding his head in agreement. It was more than I could bear. There are wounds that go deep, and the church is one of these. But of this too some other time.

Having said all that, let me add that I read with great interest the description of your home and family life. I must admit, you have a great way with words. For a moment, I placed myself into your apartment where the four of you would sit at the table, and I could smell the aroma of sauerbraten and red cabbage. And I could hear your father, the supreme man of the house, relating his stories with all the trimmings, the heel clicking, the military "Jawohl!" and the rest of it.

How utterly different my home was. Your father, a decorated officer—war, bravery, valor, wounds, pictures on the wall, and all that—you seemed to have grown up among them as content as a tadpole at the river's edge.

Let me tell you what mine was. Poverty and hoping. Two words tell nearly all of it. Ah, yes. And a lot of praying. As a young boy, thirteen and beyond, from the moment you opened your eyes—on with the donning of phylacteries, those black cubes with leather strips you put on your forehead and on your left arm, and you wind the strips around your forearm and hand, and you pray. And then some more prayers in the afternoon, again in the evening, a benediction before you eat, after you eat, before you go to bed, endless it seemed. Your house was oozing with war, mine with religion.

And there was Mama, Papa, the four children, two girls and two boys all cramped into a house—a hut is a better word—a kitchen just large enough to accommodate a clay stove and a table, a living room and one small bedroom, my parents' sanctuary. Here we fought, called for a truce when dusk set in, and the two boys had to share a single cot, and the two girls a pullout couch. And this was also the room for the most festive occasions. The holy and the profane—intertwined. Hot as an oven in the summer, freezing in the winter, pots scattered on the floor to where the ceiling leaked when it rained. Bedbugs and fleas, and there was always someone reeking of kerosene that Mama had used to get rid of head lice.

And the noise. God, how noisy the place was. You see, the front of the house was our store. A shoe store with a connecting door. As to other amenities of what you'd call civilized life, there was no running water, an outhouse leaning precariously to one side, a simple board with a hole and a reeking cesspool down below. Spiders, bees, and a swarm of buzzing flies. To this day, as I sit on a porcelain toilet in the comfort of my apartment, I'm still afraid of being bitten by a spider.

These, my dear Gerhard, were the rich Jews that your people came to plunder. The rich Jews with all that wealth they hoarded—gold, jewels, and whatnot. And even after you came and saw all that poverty, some of you were still convinced that it was only a sham, that it had to be there beneath the rotting floorboards, within the crumbling adobe walls, camouflaged of course. How ridiculous your people were, how laughable. Except, no one really laughed when *those in command of the ghetto placed levies on each community, the consequences of not coming up with their demands all too well known. And racial theories aside, plain, ordinary theft was quite high on your agenda. Racial purity, superior culture—your indoctrination, my friend, went deep, and your gullibility was bottomless.*

To get back to poverty, in our town, my family was some of the more fortunate. Many were even more poverty stricken. There was no real hunger in our house. The store kept us alive. We went to school, did our homework, and my sisters even brought home all sorts of books and hid them underneath the rafters in the attic so that Papa wouldn't find them. I too went to grade school though my father had little interest in my secular education. I don't think he ever knew what grade I was in and how well I did. Being the youngest of the lot, only Mama showed some interest in my schooling.

Poor Yakov, my older brother, a short and skinny adolescent, prematurely bald, a forehead full of pimples, shy, afraid of his own shadow, he would cringe at loud noises. And did our peasants shout as they bargained in the store, the walls thin enough for us to learn every curse word ever invented and more. And Yakov was the boy that Papa tried to teach how to run the shoe store. At the end of a market day, the peasants, usually soused by then, would come into the store, and the haggling would start, invectives, foul language. They would address Yakov as "Ty maly zhydek"—You little Jew, and some other embellishments. Yakov would shrink into himself. Finding some pretext or other, he would leave the store, sit on the stoop, and tremble like a leaf. Papa would step down to him and say, "Never mind, Yankeleh, they are just a bunch of goyim," in Yiddish of course. Papa developed a deaf ear to all the deprecations; it would wash over him like water over a stone. Yakov couldn't get used to it. And this was Yakov, my older brother, the brilliant boy when it came to the study of the Talmud, a shining light, the joy of the rabbi in our town.

And so we grew up, always one small step ahead of hunger. Living in quarters as cramped as ours, we learned to tolerate one another. We had to, or life would have been hell. And as we grew up, with all the bickering, the fighting with one another, the yelling—hard to believe, but as we grew older, we became attached to one another. Pimply Yakov, I would have gladly died for him. I nearly did. But that's another story.

Papa, Mama, strange to call them by any other name than by the Yiddish Mameh und Tateh. Tateh especially, combative, haggling and arguing with the customers in the store, ready for a fight—yet at home, soft spoken to his children. You did something to displease him, uttered a careless word, and he would simply look at you with that one eye of his, the other one, the blind, squinty one, looking at the tip of his nose. Silently, he would simply shake his head while chewing a few strands of hair from beneath his lower lip. And before you knew it, you would feel guilty. Guilt in advance for things you could have done. And Mama? No help at all. She would just stand there at the stove or at the wash basin, and she would only shrug and sometimes break out in a grin.

You'd think that now, here in America, a well-to-do man, I would think back with rancor at those years of growing up. Not at all, Gerhard, not at all. Until that ultimate catastrophe that befell us, this was home, sweet home, the memory of which would nourish me during the lonely hours of trying to bring back life to my paralyzed limbs. Nostalgia for the past, that finest antidote to when the present becomes unbearable.

I look back at what we have written to each other. It is the baring of our souls, like two strippers taking off our garments one by one, tantalizingly showing our nakedness. And we do it, and there is no audience to that spectacle. Just you and I, two crippled old men, and even stripped to our barest, does it really reveal what it was that made us the men we have become?

And I still don't know what made you, Gerhard, the young man, an apprentice to a fiddle maker, join the ranks of that infamous party of yours.

I'm getting sentimental, syrupy they call it.

Yours,
Nathan

It is four days later. His reply arrives.

Thursday, the 9th of February
Dear Nathan,

So they let me get dressed, sit at my table, strap on my pseudo leg, stand up, and take a few steps. Wobbly legs—that is one wobbly *leg, the other only a somewhat disobedient prop. I walked over to the window and longingly looked at that little patch of nature they call the garden here. There is a magnolia tree outside my window, and I keep watching the swelling of the buds. They are decidedly bigger since I left for surgery. But I could be wrong; my eyesight is getting worse even though I had a prescription for new glasses filled less than a year ago.*

And now to get back to that most unusual comparison of yours of being a stripper. A seventy-two-year-old, single-legged stripper? I laughed, a sad laugh though.

You wish to know how it all happened.

The eyes deceive. I'm speaking of those other eyes that look into the past. In time, they tend to become selective. A sort of retrospective blindness to the things we do not wish to see, searching out only those we find pleasing. But I shall do my best.

I no longer recall what it was, if anything at all, that made me different from the other youngsters. I seem to have been cast from the same mold. At least while I was still the child with the wonderment and trust in the goodness of grownups, a thing so common to all children.

As playmates, we fought with one another and then became inseparable comrades. We played soccer in some weed-overgrown yard, using stones or folded up jackets as goal posts. We hid in a remote corner of the basement of our tenement building, and there by the dim light of a basement window, we exhibited to each other our private parts, the largest one the winner and the envy of the rest of us. The girls stood on the sidewalk trying to peer into the darkened window and snickered as we emerged, apparently fully aware of what we were doing.

We were joiners. Wandervogel, a sort of Boy-Scout-equivalent youth organization. And we liked to dress alike. Short pants, knee-high socks, leather belt, and crosspiece. We learned to march as soon as we discovered our center of gravity and stood up on our hind legs. I believe we may have learned to march before walking. Even as boys going to school in the morning or coming home from school, we would fall into step and start swinging our arms.

Marching was a national habit, it seems. Father told the story of the end of World War One and the arrival of the military French occupation garrison. Each morning as they marched through the town, the military band struck up a jaunty tune. Our townsfolk on the sidewalk would soon fall into step and march along. Our good German Bürgers, the war hardly over, and the smell of gunpowder and putrid flesh still in their nostrils, and they were back to marching.

You made use of a shorthand to describe your childhood as poverty and wishing. Mine was obedience and loyalty. And yes, before I forget—punctuality. Even as a school boy, I was preoccupied with time. "Pünktlichkeit," they called it at home. But the term falls short of its real meaning. It's more than just a virtue. I chuckled reading your description and meaning of timepieces. We seemed to have been born with clocks inside our heads. Each night before retiring, and again on leaving the house to go off to work, father would wind the clock, check it against his pocket watch, a solemn ritual like the saying of a benediction, the giving thanks to the gods for having created time and then creating man for the sole purpose to see that it's kept. Even while walking to school, my eyes were riveted to the clock on the town hall spire, for there was no greater sin than being late, greater even than not having done your homework. Even later on, going to work, I had to be there on time, never a minute late.

I didn't know it then, but this preoccupation with time and punctuality became the spring for a kind of discipline and compulsiveness, a way of thinking and behaving for the rest of our lives. Pünctlichkeit, ordnung, und sauberheit—there it was, punctuality, order, and cleanliness, three indispensable virtues. Add to these a blind respect for authority, a dash of heimat— mother country, kameraderei, a pinch of feeling invincible and superior to other men, and the country was perfect for the National Socialists to sweep across like the proverbial Four Horsemen of the Apocalypse. Ever seen those movie reels showing young men dressed alike, armbands, boots, britches, belts with crosspieces, the faces full of dedication and readiness to sacrifice themselves for the great cause, never mind what the cause was? It was the togetherness, the obedience to the cause that mattered, not the essence of the cause.

Still, with all that marching and singing, I managed to grow up a quiet boy, the son of a boisterous father, a warrior derailed by the war to continuously relive it, and who could speak of little else

except of his valor and of his wounds sustained for his *Vaterland*.
I was a good student, timid though, the teacher's pet. Having to
choose between athletics or art, the latter won each time, hands
down, as they say. Obedient, by all means, a model boy, a mother's
delight. Her herzchen—her little heart. The name stuck to me, and
I resented it.

But all was not as idyllic as that. I was in my early teens when
they discovered that I had diabetes, Zuckerkrankheit they called
it. I was also flatfooted, needed glasses, a special diet, had to watch
my weight, and if that wasn't enough to set me apart from my fellow
classmates, I had to have insulin injections. It was around those years
that my father sensed that his only son was not exactly the kind to
step into his shoes, to put it mildly. I suppose he still loved me, but
I sensed that it was the kind of love one has for a child born with a
deformity.

It was at that time that the Nazi movement sprung up. Like
a whirlwind it came, demolishing the old and putting something
brand-new in its place. At first, the ranks were open to all—the
tall, the short, the chubby and the skinny, those with eyeglasses
and flat feet. As long as you wore the uniform, knew your left foot
from your right, and saluted with your outstretched arm, you were
one of them. How seductive—being just like all the others. Never
mind the diabetes, a syringe, a vial of insulin in your rucksack and
a few lumps of sugar in your pocket. In no time at all, I too became
enamored by it.

The weeding out into the pure Aryan with all the right head and body measurements came later. But in those heady days, wearing the same brand-new uniforms, marching, singing, flag waving— of course, I kept my glasses in my pocket—nearly blind without them—cut my hair short, ate the same food as everyone else, ran into trouble with my sugar levels, but it was worth it. For once in my life, I was just like the others. One of the many, the look-alike, stand-alike, be-alike. Same uniform, same stance, same countenance and composure.

I suppose the Nazi worship of the Nordic type, slim, blue-eyed, blond youth, and the ideal Nordic girl, robust, natural look, without the feminine touches of lipstick and other makeup, in essence to look like a boy, was simply the striving for sameness. And the look alike invariably led to the think alike, to that most pernicious of all features of the new man in the new Reich.

In time, anything that differed from that template of the ideal German look had to be taken out of the assembly line, thrown away, discarded as a misprint of nature, an imperfect item, the otherness. And if not eliminated altogether, at least stamped as flawed goods of lesser value.

The Jew was the extreme of that otherness. A caricature of a man depicted by the Stürmer, fleshy nose, thick lips, curly, dark hair, and so was the Gypsy with his olive-skin complexion and dark, shifty eyes, another one that didn't fit the mold. Out with him too.

You must have seen some of the pictures of those rallies. There you stood in perfect rows and columns, one of many thousands dressed alike to the smallest detail—belt buckles, sleeves rolled up to the exact same height, swastika armbands, same size, same level, shoes at high polish, even the same haircuts with a partition a la Führer. And there in front, high up on a podium against the background of eagles, stood the leaders. And they were not the ordinary earthlings. Demigods they were, looking down on you from the height of their Valhalla, extending their outstretched arm, like the high priests blessing the assembled worshipers before them. And the singing and the music. And there, in the center of the priesthood, standing on a raised podium, afloat above the multitudes, stood God himself. A forever-angry and vengeful God with a bristling mustache and a perpetual frown.

There we stood and listened. You look at the faces around you, and at first glance, you're struck by that great idealism. Idealism, my foot. Thoughts didn't matter at all. The very opposite. A total lack of it. Just empty minds, one gigantic intellectual void waiting to be filled with total, uncritical obedience of the man shrieking down at you. Don't you see, Nathan? Therein lay that blissful adoration. No need to think at all. Of anything. Empty receptacles. Dry sponges. All thoughts were transferred to the man up there on the rostrum. Simply being there, knowing that you felt and thought exactly the same way as the young men on each side, in the front and in the back of you, was the essence of that idealism.

I attended a few of these mass-worship ceremonies. How proud my father was of me, seeing me standing there in the ranks. And how proud was I of him as he marched by to the sound of blaring trumpets and I saw him in the ranks for seniors—brown uniform, boots, and britches. I truly loved him then. Son and father, now man and man. He too had that frown on his face. In fact, we all had a frown. This was serious business, the most serious I had ever experienced until then. More so than at high mass. Hitler was the master of it. Stalin, the bank robber from Tiflisi, aloft on the high wall of the Kremlin, did it too, years before Hitler. Mao Tse Tung did it decades later, but none as successfully as that once vagrant house painter from Vienna. He outdid them all.

But not all were like that. Some managed to escape that mindless conformity and submissiveness of their upbringing, that craving for uniformity. Somehow they managed to preserve some trace of individual reasoning. Hitler and his minions recognized this immediately. These were the enemy. The nonconformist.

The first order of business was to do some house cleaning Nazi style, of course. "Rassereinheit," that pernicious doctrine of racial purity, came only later. At first, those who could think for themselves and had the courage to say so had to be done away with—the clergy, writers, teachers, artists, and of course the Jews, that pernicious creed with their nasty habit of individual reasoning for themselves.

I wish I could say that I was one of those who did not succumb to that allure of conformity. No, my dear Nathan, I fell in love with it. Head over heels, as they say.

Having said this, having laid bare the German psyche as I see it now, it's peculiarities, all the falsehood and pretense, Germany, my friend—and here I must make another confession—after all that I said, Germany is still home. I don't know how you feel about your Poland, but I would not be surprised to learn that you too, as you reminisce of the past, think of it as home.

It seems that all immigrants, whether they leave on their own accord in search for a better life, or they are compelled to leave for whatever reason, carry somewhere deep down in their bundles and suitcases a good dose of nostalgia for the place where they were born and raised. Having left it, in time they think of it as the biblical Garden of Eden. Forgetting the serpent, they think back on it wistfully, like the babe longing for its mother's loving arms, for the time when all was good and forgiving, and they dream of going back, if only for a glimpse of that paradise, not necessarily the one they left, and more likely the one they would have wished it to be.

Don't misunderstand me. I love America, but I was never fully at home here. I had my own shop, lived in a fine apartment, felt safe and secure, really secure without having to prove my manhood and allegiance at every step. But home was elsewhere.

You spoke of your home, a village—I know. I was there. In comparison, my home wasn't that bad. Still, it was far from opulence. It was a third-floor walk-up apartment in a tenement house in an alley off the main street in Frankfurt. A steep, cobblestone paved street led to it, the gutters forever wet and smelly, an inconspicuous entrance door with a small number on a ceramic plate, chipped and grime-covered, the staircase reeking of cat, but once inside, there was the window, and if you leaned out, you could see down below the River Main flowing slowly, changing color with the season and the times of the day.

Years later, here in America on Christmas days, sitting on the floor, bracing my two little nephews as they sang "Holy Night," I found myself drifting along the same melody, except mine was "Heilige Nacht." And the same on Easter Sunday in church. I would be transported back to that small church around the corner where I lived, with its cold stone floor and uncomfortable wooden benches and the old Pfarrer, Herr Krämer, droning on in his cracked voice and pronounced lisp. Home was the place where at day's end I would go for a walk along the river, and the place where I furtively kissed a girl for the first time.

And even now, while living here in the lap of luxury that America so generously offers to its newcomers, I still am thrilled at the sound of an older man and his wife standing at the bus station speaking German. For all I know, the sound of the German language may be grating to your ear, and who could blame you? But you, my friend, wanted to know who I am, and having once resolved to be as truthful as possible, perhaps for the first time since arriving in this country, I'm telling it to you along with so many other things I never dared to tell anyone.

In that duet of ours of baring our souls, is America really your home? Don't you dream of being back there where you were young and—shall we use that trite word—innocent?

Yours,
Gerhard

P.S. My foot feels warmer, though parts of it still lack sensation, especially the great toe. But the middle one, I stubbed it the other day—did it ever hurt. And not long ago, it was completely numb. I clasped it in my hand and laughed my head off. Can you imagine? Rejoicing over a painful toe?

Gerhard

CHAPTER
22

I READ GERHARD'S LETTER, ANGER welling up in me with each successive sentence. I feel a new wave of animosity toward the man. I put the pages down, wishing I never read its content. Wondering if I may have read into it things that weren't there, I thumb through pages once again. But they are there, and the gulf between us, gradually narrowing these past few months, stands gaping wide once again. I never saw those Nazi rallies, not while they took place, but how many times have I seen them in the movies now, how often on television—these torch parades, the singing, the martial music, the hobnailed boots beating out a rhythm, a brutal rhythm of a song of conquest and destruction. And now, more than ever, I see him as part of it. Damn him, why did he have to describe it so vividly? I can see him now, Gerhard the gangly youth with his arm stretched out in that mindless salute. Gerhard with a cudgel running down the street along with other thugs, their sticks landing on the backs and heads of old men and women fleeing in terror. And as I reread parts of his letter, simple words turn into shouts, their shouts, his shouts, the vicious jeering, *"Jude, Jude!"*

In my mind, I have seen these scenes again and again. They are the stuff of which my nightmares are made, but now they all come rushing back at me relentlessly, like unstoppable tidal waves. I see him there, one of the many in that stampede of evil. He and his father are there, for all I know his pious *Mutti*, one more German *Hausfrau* flanking the streets of their beloved Frankfurt am Main, shrieking wildly, *"Heil Hitler,"* with their arms stretched out to the motorcade of the Führer having come for a visit. There they stand before my eyes with their arms outstretched, palms extended not to greet, just to touch the very air through which that monster of all time was passing.

No, I wish I hadn't read the letter.

There is a soft knock on the door. "May I come in?"

She enters carrying an aluminum cane with a rubber-tipped tripod. "Tomorrow, if you like, we could just try walking with it." She nods at the crutch and hesitates for a moment. "Just a few steps. Maybe just to stand up, no?"

My not-too-subtle matchmaker places it right next to the wheelchair and hesitates before leaving, waiting for me to acknowledge her offering, but I just finished reading his letter and am in no mood to walk. Not to where she so obviously intends me to walk. She leaves shaking her head, and I'm glad to be left alone to watch and wait for the day to end. The wind whips the single branch against the windowpane, and it sounds like a knock on the window by an invisible hand to rouse me from my rumination that is slowly drifting into another nightmare.

I turn on the light. Gerhard's letters lay scattered on the table, and I place them neatly into a single pile. I can use my left hand now to flatten the pages and place them, letter by letter, between the jaws of the stapler. Quite a pile now, the last one on the top, the first one at the bottom. A man's lifetime rests here between the first letter with its calligraphic *"Dear Mr. Klein ... this is surely the most difficult letter I have ever written,"* and now, speaking of his joining those unsavory ranks, he tells me, *"No, my dear Nathan, I fell in love with it. Head over heels, as they say."*

I flip the pages, scanning the headings. For a long time, it's "Dear Mr. Klein" before addressing me as "Dear Friend," soon followed by "Dear Nathan." My eyes fall on the page of one letter: *"Suddenly I felt as an intruder. That I had no right being here."* The man was writing about his travel to Jerusalem and then describing his visit to the Yad Vashem. *"I walked on and wept. Others wept too. That's about all I could do, weep and let the tears run down my face without wiping them."* And then, by way of apology, he writes, *"You, at least, have someone to share with all those troubling visions. I have no one."*

If I could only bridge the gap between that saluting,

Jew-hating, *Hitler Jugend* and the one-legged, old man sitting in a room in one of the nearby buildings, some of the windows already lit. I would like to fuse these two men into one, but I cannot. There are still two of them, and I cannot make them link arms to become a single one capable of hating and loving, perhaps with an equal passion and intensity. Why must they stand so far apart, the young one who mockingly puts a lie to the older.

No, I'm not the forgiving kind. Not even half as much as I would like to be.

With both hands firmly planted on the table, and shifting my weight forward, I can now raise myself from my chair. I can stand now but dare not take my hands away, especially the left, the unsteady one. I reach for Miss Hedberg's new gift of a cane she providentially placed within my reach. It's there, cool to the touch, soothingly cool, comforting, and inviting as if it has been there all along and waiting for my hand. I grip the handle and try to shift my weight, but I veer. My heart begins to race, and beads of sweat sprout on my forehead. But I'm up now. I stand, both hands grasping the edge of the table, and I slowly inch myself toward the window. The light inside is reflected in the windowpanes, and I turn off the table lamp, plunging the room into darkness. Only the many lit windows faintly illuminate the garden and the path below. Rows and rows of lit windows, two floors high, blue, yellow, red, the television lights flicker like bulbs in a penny arcade. So many here. So many of the pained and destitute, and so many of the forgotten, the no longer wanted.

Emma Lazarus and her sonnet comes to mind, and her words engraved on the pedestal of that Great Lady: *"Give me your tired, your poor, your huddled masses ... the wretched refuse ... I lift my lamp beside the golden door."* Will there be another Emma to raise another lamp for those wretched already here, now huddled in their rooms waiting and waiting, and no longer knowing what it is they are waiting for?

I recall a cold night like this when my ship sailed into the harbor. The Statue of Liberty was shrouded in fog, and I couldn't see her. I kept dreaming of her during the many years of waiting to board a ship on the way to America. Dream days of gazing into the distance, sighting land on the horizon, and at last seeing her standing in the midst of a calm sea, arm raised against a pristine sky in a welcome gesture, the modern colossus, not to guard the harbor, but to salute the arrivals. But she wasn't there that night to greet me or to greet all the others on board who stood on deck peering into the fog-shrouded darkness, seeing nothing and listening to the strange sounds of foghorns conversing with one another, and trying to decipher that strange language, those first sounds from the promised land reaching our ears. I didn't see her that night, but I saw her later. Many times.

Emma Lazarus, the infirm, the helpless, the darkness outside—I am gripped by morbid thoughts, wrapped in a mourner's veil, this one brought on by having drifted into the past—a dead-end street. Why did I ever gaze down at that bench in the garden, at that old man, a conduit from the now into the then, the past like a hidden reef forever threatening the unwary?

I reach for the pen, that new remedy of mine, a tranquilizer, a soother of aches for my past and present maladies.

Monday, the 13th of February
Dear Gerhard,

It took me a long time to get acquainted with the image of that Gerhard you wrote about. For lack of a better term, let me call him Gerhard the First, the one I'm writing to now being Gerhard the Second. I must confess—it wasn't easy, and I still have trouble switching back and forth from one to the other like one of those swinging pendulums in my clocks. To go from one to the other is a little like getting out of a comfortable, warm bath and plunging into icy waters. I'm still shivering. The fact that Gerhard the First was one of many millions who participated in that insanity doesn't endear him to my heart any more than the warriors of those Mongol hordes who invaded my native Poland in the twelfth and thirteenth centuries,

*laying siege and slaughtering towns and hamlets indiscriminately.
But give me time.*

*I promise, though, to try to keep at arm's length that first Gerhard
and think only of the one that informs me of a stubbed toe and how
jubilant he was feeling pain. One good leg and one good foot and how
you rejoice. It takes one like me to understand it. A short while ago,
I too went into a state of rapture over the use of my leg. Trying to
walk, I put my leg down, shifted my full weight on it, and it held. I
let out a shout of joy when it happened. Imagine, two old men, very
old men, one being glad that his toe hurts, and the other that he can
stand on his own leg. There is something absurd, almost ridiculous
about it. If only it weren't so tragic. Let us rejoice while we can.*

*The other day, I too looked at a single branch near my window—
not much else to look at in this wintry panorama—and I too saw the
buds swelling. Any day now, any day, and there'll be spring again.
You'll have your bench, your outdoor residence beside this walled-in
existence of ours. And who knows, one of these sunny days I might
even join you there, though I must admit, I have never been much
of a sun worshiper or an outdoors man.*

*I read with interest your description of your days of carefree
tramping through the woods, Wandervogel, you called it. Uniforms,
mandolin, singing—how utterly different from my childhood. I
too liked to go for a stroll into the woods. The forest, a dense one,
stretching for kilometers in all directions was right there at the edge
of our hamlet. Living close by, a short walk only, it held less allure to*

us than to those youngsters living in the city. It was a place to gather berries, to get bellyaches from gorging on them, and to find refuge when things went wrong, when your heart was about to break and you wanted to cry unseen by others. Whatever moments there were of joy and exuberance in tromping through the woods, the way you described it, they have been long since erased by those tragic years that followed, the ones you and I knew so well, especially the time when that forest became a refuge for the few of us who managed to run away on the morning of the carnage.

But that is a long story. A tragic story, painful to even write about. One that should not mar the rapture of two old men having discovered the joy of standing upright on their own legs.

Perhaps some other time.

Yours,
Nathan

P.S. I'm struck by how often we end our letters with a note, "It's a long story—some other time." You would think we have all the time in the world and there is no need to hurry.

CHAPTER
23

"Shall we try?" Miss Hedberg nods at the cane. "Just a few steps at a time."

She watches intently as I take my first step. I do it, like a child getting up on his hind legs for the first time, one hand grasping the cane handle, the other stretched forward. But she is there, her arm a protective half-circle, an embrace wide enough to let me be free, yet close enough to catch me.

"One, and two, and three, and one more, just one more, Mr. Klein." She counts and claps her hands.

I'm upright. I can look down at my feet and stand on the polished floor, and I can lift my feet, put my entire weight on them. They are mine now. I, their righteous owner, have repossessed them. What triumph, as if the past was nothing more than a stepping stone, a prelude in my long journey back to be the man I was. Tired, I finally get back into the wheelchair and gaze contemptuously at the footrest, the side arms, the wheels that served me so well until now.

Before leaving my room, Miss Hedberg reaches for the letter I wrote last night and stashes it into her pocket.

"Well, well, Mr. Klein. One surprise after another. Look at the way you're handling the crutch." Miss Hedberg is full of flattery this morning.

"Cane, Miss Hedberg. It's a cane, an ordinary cane with some adjustable metal knobs, not a crutch." I correct her with a mock frown.

"I beg your pardon, Mr. Klein. A cane it is. And judging by the way you are using it, we have been practicing, perhaps?"

"Perhaps."

"Chomping at the bits, your friend Gerhard cannot wait to be allowed to leave his room and go down into the garden. Cold and unfriendly, the weather." She goes on chatting and pushing the empty wheelchair while I walk slowly. "Just in case," she says and nods at the squeaky wheelchair.

"I think I'm ready to join him there."

"Not alone, you don't."

"So little confidence, Miss Hedberg, so little confidence."

"Never trust little children and old men." She nods and holds the door open to the treatment room.

"Today we shall learn to walk without looking at our feet." She hands me the controversial cane-crutch. "And, Mr. Klein, you don't have to close your eyes." Her voice changes again from the jocular to the schoolmarm kind. "Now, keep them open but look straight ahead, not down on the floor. Now, don't be afraid; the floor will not tilt to the left. And one, and two, and three, and …" She goes on counting with clapping her hands. She is wrong though, for the floor does tilt, and I do lose the grip on my cane and fall into the embrace of her outstretched arms.

It's a day of trying to walk on my own, grasping the handle of my cane too firmly, and watching a small blister form near the base of my thumb, the skin having gone soft from lack of use. Perhaps I could visit him. The thought of seeing him has been germinated slowly, and yet I find myself hesitating. I shall go, but not until I can walk, stand straight, chin up, steady as a rock, and look at the man at eye-to-eye level, unafraid of veering to one side. Is it my pride, I wonder, or am I still afraid of the man, not of Gerhard the one-legged fiddle maker with a sore toe, but of the other one, the unwanted, the uninvited visitor of my nightmares of so many years now?

CHAPTER
24

AN ENTIRE WEEK HAS gone by without a letter. Perplexed, I find myself gazing at Miss Hedberg's pocket—empty, like her face each time our eyes meet. She seems apprehensive and clearly not in the mood to speak about Gerhard. Her uneasiness is contagious, and the perennial worrier in me conjures up the worst.

At last, a letter in her pocket. No smile though.

Monday, the 20th of February
Dear Nathan,

Forgive the delay. How discouraging. Just when all seemed to be going well, another problem shakes its ugly head. Thrombosis, they call it. In laymen's terms—clogged. This time it's a vein in my leg. After all the things that happened to me, I'm a walking medical dictionary. And so I'm confined to staying in bed, my only companion a radio. Dismal days just as the icicles hanging from the eaves above my window are beginning to melt, some crashing to the ground below with the sound of shattering glass, the surest sign that spring is not far off. And I so hoped to be able to hobble down to that bench of mine, my other residence, as you call it.

My next-door resident, a man with severe Parkinson's disease, calls me the sun worshiper. Henry Eisen is his name. Once in a while, he knocks on the door and enters. "Anything I can do for you, Gerhard? I'm going to the front office." Most of the time, Eisen forgets what he intended to do by the time he reaches the door. Poor man, he can hardly hold a cup without spilling its contents all over himself. The walls separating our rooms must have been made of cardboard, and his visitors, either his wife or sister—the shrillest voices you ever heard—no sooner does the door close, and she would ask him, "Nu, vos tut der meshugene Deitscher?"—What is the crazy German doing? The resemblance to the German language and my proximity to Jewish people in my neighborhood, I can follow their conversation without missing many words. After all these years, I'm still the meshugene Deitscher—the crazy German.

Strange, but I'm not a sun worshiper. I simply hate confined spaces. Alone in a room, the doors and windows closed, is enough to throw me into a state of panic. Claustrophobia they call it. A terrible affliction for one having to spend so much time in bed. And *so every opportunity I get to be out there, I grab it, no matter what the weather. I bundle myself up, and there I sit and dream with my eyes closed. It wasn't always this bad, but year after year, it seems to have gotten worse. And then another thing happened. To get away from walls closing in on me, I used to go out on the balcony of my apartment. One day I looked down and broke out in a cold sweat. The street down below, the handrail I was clutching, the horizon, it all began spinning, and I had the feeling of being hurled into the air and over the side of the balcony. I never dared to go out there again. It turned out to be one more phobia, this one by the fancy name of acrophobia. There are more; in fact, I'm full of phobias. But don't let me bore you with listing the lot of them.*

I shouldn't be writing this. I'm in a foul mood, sullen, depressed, anything but given to writing letters, even to you, my friend. You have enough problems without having to read the outpouring of a heavy heart. Sometimes I wonder if I will ever be well enough to be out there on that bench of mine. Lying on my back, leg up again, staring at the ceiling, at that nondescript void up there, I wonder if all that has been happening to me is not some divine retribution for things I have done to others, or failed to do when I should have. I know, you will laugh reading this, you the nonbeliever that you are, and think of it as just so much dribble of a self-pitying old man. And for all I know, you could be right.

I read you last letter, and my eyes became arrested by your reference to the forest having been a refuge for the few who managed to escape from that tragedy. It's your first reference to how you survived, and I can well understand the pain you must feel writing about it. I often wondered how it happened, and sensing how difficult it must be for you to write about it, I refrained from asking. It was the forest then. Dear God, the forest near the outskirt of the town, so close and no doubt within sight and earshot of what was happening in the ghetto on that fateful day.

My mind reels as I try to conjure up what agony it must have been for you to hear and, for all I know, to see what was happening in the ghetto on that day. Though I never sought refuge in a forest, I can imagine the hardship you must have endured hiding in it, and if I recall, it was autumn, with cold weather approaching.

Let me add here that I know that forest quite well. In a perverse way, it also served me as a place of refuge, though it would be a mockery to compare mine with yours. On a warm summer day, I used to go there for a pleasant walk just to get away from the squalor of the ghetto and sit there and dream of being back home. There's something ubiquitous about forests wherever you encounter them. They whisper the same universal language, exude the same aroma of pine sap, spread the same soft carpet of needles beneath your feet, and so I went there seeking an island of home. And there I would sit on some stump of a tree in the forest of Kostowa and dream of the Taunus forest on the outskirts of Frankfurt. Child-like dreaming with my gun-toting belt unbuckled and at my feet, the tunic unbuttoned, the treetops converging above me like spires of a cathedral, a place untouched by war, by strife, by walls, and of course, dreaming of Esta and all the tragedy that seemed to loom ahead, for her, for the unborn child, for all of us.

I promise to be more diligent in my correspondence, but this damned leg of mine.

Yours,
Gerhard

Wednesday the 22nd of February
Dear Gerhard,

Sorry about that thrombosis. Add your affliction to mine, and we could be Job of biblical lore.

A while ago, I looked out the window. The sun shone its brightest this winter yet. The bench stood there, wet, glistening, and provoking. Don't lose heart. Before you know it, you'll be sitting there, heavy coat, shawl, gloves, birds in the sky, and birds on the walkway waiting to be thrown some crumbs.

It's almost eerie that you and I should meet nearly half a century after having sought refuge in the same forest, though for different reasons, mine to save my life, yours to find a few moment of solitude. Still, we were there, perhaps sitting on the same moss-covered tree stump right next to the path. Another shared experience, similar to walking on the same cracked sidewalk of the ghetto, you glaring down on us, and we averting our eyes. Our being here together under the same roof has all the making of a macabre tragedy, the plot convoluted, the roles of hero and villain shifting back and forth just to amuse the gods, though I really don't believe that God, mine or yours, had anything to do with it. If there were gods, they couldn't be this cruel.

You guessed right. It was the forest. But before that came the destruction of thousands of souls. A single day it was, and it overshadowed the many years of humiliation and pain that preceded it and all that followed afterward. It was a day that began at dawn and ended long before dusk, and in that short span of time, so many lives were snuffed out. Some were killed on the spot, others were chased out of town to be done away with elsewhere, and a number of those hardy and without children were shipped away, as I later found out.

It was shortly after dawn when they arrived. It rained, a drizzle, more like a mist. How many times have I relived that day of utter madness. Even now, trying to write about it, something within me reins in my thoughts as if afraid of stumbling upon things concealed even from myself. And something within me bids me to halt, to cease recalling those dread-filled moments when I was convinced that death was imminent, that I may never see the end of the day. They arrived in a salvo of gunfire, and there were none who mistook it for anything other than the end we had all anticipated but so fervently hoped would never happen in this little hamlet of ours, a shtetle we called it, hidden away in the hinterlands of Poland.

Startled from a sound sleep by gunfire, I ran. Panic-stricken, I grabbed my heavy overcoat and ran out of the house without a moment's hesitation. I had no plans, no destination except to get away from those men surrounding us, the skull and crossbones insignias on their hats leaving little doubt of what they intended to do. I ran—a wild dash into narrow alleys, between houses, through broken-down fences, away from them, away from the sound of shooting, the sound of bullets ricocheting all around me, and away from screams. And there on the horizon, not far away was the forest.

How I got there is only a dim memory of running, gasping for air, the narrow path leading uphill, stumbling and getting back on my feet, being frightened out of my wits, a kind of fear I had never experienced in my life. I ran, giving no thought to anything else but to gain distance from what was going on around me. It was only later, after having reached the forest's edge and making a dash into the low growth, my face pressed into the mossy ground and gasping for air, that I remembered that I ran out of the house without saying a parting word. I ran and left them all behind without casting a glance to what was happening to them, to all the others.

Concealed by the heavy foliage, I stayed there for most of the day, occasionally daring to raise my head to glimpse at the town below, afraid to go back, unwilling to enter deeper into the forest, as if the sight of the town was the one and only anchor that still tethered me to those I had left behind. I stayed there riveted to the moist ground until day's end when the sound of gunfire ceased and the groaning of departing military trucks faded in the distance. The butchery had ceased. Another victory for that glorious Reich that you, Gerhard, were so proud of as a young man.

At last I dared to stand up and see the entire span of the valley spread below me. It was the longest sunset of my life. Smoke had risen above the rooftops, a thin veil spread over the town like a venomous embrace. A windless day, it hovered above the thatched roofs as if tethered down by invisible threads. How I wished for darkness to blot it out, to put an end to a day so painful. At the same time, I wished for the day to last, for darkness carried a finality, an erasure of all those lives irretrievably lost from sight.

It was a crimson sunset, the sun clutching to the edge of the horizon and then slowly dipping into a brown haze. A sunset befitting the day about to pass. It was a sunset to mar the beauty of so many other sunsets that followed, and to this day, I can still see it. I sat at the forest's edge until the first lights went on in the windows. Those in the ghetto remained unlit. None were left to turn them on. Then came the night. I'd been to the forest many times before but never at night, and this one was full of menacing shadows and noises.

In one of your previous letters, you mentioned having gone away and returning a day, or was it two days later. I too returned, but it was many days later. Shielded by darkness, I dared to leave the forest and went back to catch a glimpse of what happened, still hoping that I might find someone still alive. I reached the narrow lanes of the ghetto. Keeping to the shadows, I walked on tiptoe. I whispered names into still-open windows, smashed doors. Occasionally, I stood still, hoping to catch a glimpse of life, the creaking of a door, footsteps other than mine. My worst fears were confirmed. There was nothing there but an eerie stillness, each hut like a grave in the old cemetery. On moonless nights, I ventured down again and again—it was always the same.

You tell me that all these years you went on believing that your Esta may have survived somehow, and you tell me that you have never given up hope. Well, my friend, neither have I. For the longest time afterward, I went on fantasizing that some survived. Perhaps driven away, they managed to endure, or escape, or be spared, and some day we may be reunited with one another. And even now, half a century later, I indulge in that childish luxury of daydreaming and make-believe that some made it, and one of these days the telephone will ring, or a letter will arrive.

But to get back to my hiding in that cursed forest. Menacing as it was, especially during that first night, there was no other place to hide. How murky those woods, how threatening with that monotone whisper in the treetops, how frightening that sudden dull thump of a falling pinecone hitting the softly carpeted forest floor. And at daybreak when darkness lifted and the sun shone again, the light and shadows playing between the trees—there always seemed to be a man behind me. The bellow of a wounded animal, the hooting of an owl, the shriek of a hare, like a child frightened in its sleep, it was enough to make me break out in a cold sweat.

For a while, I was convinced that I was the only one who managed to get away. But I was mistaken. There were four of us, as unlikely a foursome you could have thrown together to survive in a forest. The oldest, Shmuel was his name, a man in his fifties. I knew him vaguely as an intensely pious man, a father of a brood of children, his wife a haggard woman forever standing in front of her house, selling fruit from their little garden while Shmuel would spend most of the day in the study room in the back of the synagogue studying Talmudic texts. Shmuel, the pious Talmud scholar, couldn't tell one end of an ax from the other. All we ever asked him to do was to keep the embers of our concealed fire alive so we wouldn't freeze, and even at that, he kept falling asleep. Matches—those still dry were a fast-dwindling item. Fresh ones were difficult to find while groping in the empty houses at night. The other two were young men, twin brothers, twenty-one years old. They lived for each other only, oblivious to the two of us, though they did share whatever meager bits of food we could gather.

Concealed by the trees and underbrush, we'd approach the edge of the forest and wait for dusk to arrive. Like men at a wake, we would sit in our concealment and gaze at the town down below. Silence most of the time except for the thump-thump sound of threshers in some barn, the mooing of a cow, the barking of dogs. This was our town we had run away from, and having to look at it from a distance only made my heart contract. Our town, and here we sat, the four of us, sometimes only the three, Shmuel staying behind to tend the fire. At first, the town seemed so near, but as time went on and we realized *that we could not go back there, the distance seemed to grow larger with each passing day, then weeks and finally months.*

In time, our clothes were in tatters, and our boots were wrapped in pieces of burlap sacks to keep warm and to keep the wetness out. How cold it became the moment the sun went down, the trees perpetually casting a shade, and the ground soggy and dank. After a while, our gloves wore out, and we had to wrap our hands in whatever rags we could find. Four scarecrows we were, unshaven, grimy, hungry, afraid to make a large fire to warm ourselves, let alone to heat up a bit of water. Filled with hate and envy, we ventured to the edge of the forest and watched the town down below us, the lights in the windows, the smoke spiraling from chimneys while the four of us were dying of hunger and cold. And the people down there, the good Christians, once our neighbors, could walk and speak, could stand by the fence to have a chat with their neighbors while we were frightened of our own shadows. Without relief. A broken twig, a pinecone falling to the ground, the screeching of a bird on its perch, the mistaking our own footsteps for those of another person perhaps in pursuit of us.

I read somewhere about hardship and common danger bonding men. Another fairytale. We didn't hate one another, the four of us, but whatever transpired there during those six months while each one of us was nursing his own wounds, it was not friendship. We spoke to one another, grunts most of the time. One tried to reminisce about a thing or two about the most recent past, and three pairs of eyes would bore into him like daggers. The catastrophe that befell us became a taboo subject. I suppose the wounds were too raw. In fact, even later, long after the Russians came, we still couldn't speak of what happened.

There were moments of elation and moments of despair. We'd sit in our dugout hunched over the little fire, a pot with some vegetables—potatoes, turnips, onions, things we could steal from the fields below or left for us by one lonely farmer living on the outskirts of the town. He would throw it over the stone fence and pretend he didn't know how it vanished in the middle of the night. There were other occasions when our spirits lifted beyond the pall of gloom. Suddenly the stillness of the night would be broken by a distant rumble that sounded like thunder. We would raise our eyes to the little, open space between the treetops and wait for it to happen again in the vain hope that it was Russian artillery, the front surely getting closer, any day now, God willing. We would sit up, remain silent, and wait for the sound to become louder. And so we would sit like this for hours, chewing on a twig or on a stem of a leafy weed to still the hunger, and wait.

I chuckled as I read your description of that wondrous aroma of pine resin and the damp softness of the forest floor, light playing in the swaying treetops, and the many things to delight the senses. To the four of us in search of shelter, the forest became a curse. Like moles, we burrowed underneath that softness as we sat there huddled over a small fire—God forbid someone might notice the smoke in the distance. Our eyes were stinging and tearing, the niggardly heat and our clothes forever damp. How I grew to hate that forest. It was hell. To this day, I still tend to draw away from a crackling fireplace and dried pinecones exploding in the fire.

After the war was over, I learned of other towns where the same mayhem took place, where some fled the way we did. A few found roaming bands of other refugees, obtained weapons, fought back, their stories of daring approaching the legendary. But not I, Gerhard. I was no great hero. All I had was a rusty kitchen knife one of us found during one of those nightly forays for something to eat. Although I have a tendency to conjure up all kinds of feats of bravery, and like a child with his wishful thinking in which I am the all-powerful Nathan, I have to confess that I never was the fighting kind. Argue, fisticuff fights—yes, argue endlessly—yes, but to kill another human being, plunge a bayonet into another man's belly, was unthinkable. Our way to survive was to plead, cajole, bribe, use any means available, fair or foul, as they say. Or we ran and hid in the single hope to see the sun rise on another day. But never kill.

Speaking of sunrise, I just looked at my clock. It's nearly three o'clock in the morning, and my eyes feel as if someone has thrown a handful of sand into my face.

Soon another day.

Nathan

CHAPTER
25

The stillness of the night is marred by hurried footsteps down the corridor, the slamming of doors, a muffled voice, inarticulate but with a distinct note of urgency. The footsteps fade, car doors are being slammed, a motor is being revved, then silence again. I close my eyes, hoping for sleep to stem the flow of my narrative. But like a river that spills over the banks at flood time, my raking up past events continues unbridled long after I have folded the pages, stashed them in the envelope, and written Gerhard's name in my customary large-block print.

I sleep poorly. I dream—my dreams my unwanted companions. I always do after a journey into the past, as if trapped there. I close my eyes, and like an afterglow, the images continue. The forest is there. From a distance, the town looks so deceptively calm and serene, but I need not cup my ear to hear the volleys of gunfire ripping through the still air, and I know the reapers, and I know their harvest.

And like flipping the pages in a picture book, once again I relive my groping through the dense forest, the stumbling over a log felled a long time ago, the trunk rotten and covered with slippery moss. Whipped across the face by an overhanging branch, my cheek is set aflame, and I soon become aware that my face is wet. I wipe it. It's sticky. I taste it—salty. I'm bleeding. And suddenly I find myself falling, the ground giving beneath my feet and all of me plunging into some abysmal hole filled with decaying leaves and muddy soil. And there is always someone following me who keeps on doing so until I recognize the echo of my own footsteps reverberating through the darkness like a daytime shadow.

I feel myself running. I see the tree trunks alongside keeping pace with my flight. Men, they seem, other men following me, chasing me, peasants, Germans. My legs seem leaden, as they usually are in that state of half-dream, half-wakefulness, but I know that I must get away, run to where the forest looms at its darkest, where it holds the promise to engulf and conceal me, where there is safety. I still feel myself running, but the darkness is only illusive and never dark enough for me to stop, to rest and feel safe. At last a ditch, soft ground, deep shadows, the gurgling of water splashing down a rock. Peace. I'm down where there is wetness and concealment, and I close my eyes and weep.

I'm alone, utterly alone in that forest, and frightened of my solitude. For just one moment, the trees cease swaying while I keep whispering into the shadows, "Are you there? Anybody there?" but I receive no reply. And suddenly they materialize. I see them in my half-dream, half-awake state the way I did on the third day of hiding, convinced by then that I was the only one left. A recurrent apparition. Three men stand in a small clearing. I see them standing there the way I saw them then and so many times since. Three statues as if sculpted in stone, and I stop there, not daring to move. Then one of them slowly moves his head and peers into the shadows where I am concealed and where I stepped on a twig.

My people, black hats, black kaftans, muddy, one has his sleeve torn down the length. Unshaven, the pale face of one is mud-streaked, or is it clotted blood? They are as frightened at the sound of the snapping twig, frightened as I am. At last I dare to show my face, unafraid that they will run away and I will be alone once more. I step back, and none of us are glad or sad of being only four and no one else. No, I reply, I too have no food, and no, I wasn't there to see if anyone was still alive, and no, I haven't come across others. And the four of us stand in the small clearing resigned to being the only ones who made it to safety.

There is cold, and there is hunger in that dream-born state of reliving those moments. And even now I can still feel the maddening pangs of hunger, the moist, enticing tree bark, the irresistible urge to sink my teeth into it, only to spit it out, the tartness lingering in my mouth. And the numbing cold; no amount of blowing my breath against my fingers and wrists seems to rekindle a trace of warmth. Or the rains, wind-driven, lashing without mercy while I search for a spot of dryness beneath the canopy of a tree, and finally giving up, letting myself slide down and leaning against a tree trunk, letting it come, no longer caring if I live or die. And the snow, the bitter cold and the four of us huddled against a small flame concealed between three boulders, the four of us clinging to the ground, our arms stretched out to catch the bits of warmth, and like highway robbers, we have our kerchiefs pulled up over the faces against the acrid smoke. Against the blackness of the night, their faces, dimly illumined by the flames, stand out, their eyes staring at the flames as if in a trance. The little fire—glowing embers most of the time, it captures their gaze, for there is nothing else to gaze at in that pitiful hideout. And there is nothing to say to one another, each quietly nurturing his own sorrow.

The older man, Reb Shmuel, a Talmudic scholar, once in a while speaks silently, only his lips moving, his eyes gazing unblinkingly at the fire. The twins speak. But they have a language of their own, a word here, then another one, a shrug of a shoulder, a nod—I cannot understand them, but I don't really care. They live in a world inaccessible to the rest of us.

And so huddled, we sit at arm's length from each other and yet worlds apart.

I let the curtain fall. A blessed sleep that erases the last flickering images, and there is calm at last.

I must have slept soundly, for on awakening, the sun is high. The letter I wrote before falling asleep is gone. She must have been here and, finding me sound asleep, took it.

Monday, the 27th of February
Dear Friend,

How painful that story of your stay in the forest. Reading it helped me to forget my own pain in that swollen and throbbing leg of mine, even when it is raised. They say another week, perhaps two. The doctor came, looked at it, and hinted at sending me back to the hospital. I flatly refused. And so I stayed in bed. There are days that leave behind an indelible mark, and there are others, time-stood-still days like these past few, and they vanish as if they never happened.

You mentioned having gone back into the ghetto in search for some survivors. Strange coincidences, the two us having walked through those empty streets, passed the same lifeless houses, peered into doors and windows left ajar. I was there in daytime, and you, afraid to show yourself, went there at night. You must have wept in sorrow, and I did the same, though also in shame.

I returned to the comfort of my new lodgings in my next

assignment, feeling pity and remorse, while you must have endured a kind of suffering that must be hard to describe. October the fifth it was when the ghetto was liquidated, and if I remember correctly, the Russian Army did not reach these parts until the next year sometimes in March. Nearly six month of agony. It must have been sheer hell. Not only the part of finding food and shelter, but being there in hiding at the edge of the town where you once lived, and now in close proximity to the many who died.

I try to imagine the moment of deliverance on seeing the Russians on the horizon, but this too is difficult to perceive for anyone who has not gone through your torments.

Please, write. As often as you can.

Gerhard

Wednesday, the 1st of March
Dear Gerhard,

Spring is here at last. It happened almost overnight. The spindle-shaped magnolia buds exploded into a riot of lavender. Joy to my senses as I open the window and inhale the fragrance of steaming soil and see the mounds of earth, swollen and ready to give birth to the first spring flowers. Unfortunately, it must be tantalizing to you, who so much loves the outdoors, "away from enclosing walls," as you called it, to be cooped up and your leg still painful.

It seems we are destined to meet each other through these pages only. But some day, some day we will meet—I refuse to give up. Our postman hinted at wheeling myself, or wobbling over to your room for just a visit, but somehow I cannot do it. I don't quite know why, but I had my heart set on the two of us meeting down in the garden, on that bench of yours, perhaps in time becoming a bench of ours, but not until then. So get well, Gerhard, and don't wait too long.

You guessed right when you said that life in a forest, most of it during a cold autumn and a freezing winter, was hell. As I think back, it seems that it was always night; at least those were the moments most deeply etched in my mind. Darkness, a hole in the ground, the rotting stump of a fallen tree, thick roots like a thousand snakes feasting on the decay and putrefaction, the stench of wilt, the odor of my own sweat and that of the others huddled nearby. The intoxicating aroma of Mother Earth, *I read somewhere, I don't recall where now. Aroma? Intoxicating? Who wrote this must have been out for a walk in the woods with a blanket to sit on and a basket of delicatessen to munch on in the company of friends.*

We lived on the edge of a dead town, you wrote. True, but it was our part of the town that died, not theirs. They, the Christian townspeople went on with their lives the way they did for a thousand years or longer. And while we silently watched from a distance, they went on with their harvesting and winter plowing as if nothing had happened. The church bells rang as they always did. Lit Christmas trees were visible through the windows. The horse-driven carts had given to sleighs with bells, and the occasional spirals of smoke issuing

241

from chimneys had become billowy. It all went on as we, who had lived there for as long as anyone could remember, had only been an interlude, trespassers, now evicted and gotten rid of once and forever.

How did we survive? As I think back, I too wonder. I suppose you could say by the skin of our teeth. No heroics, just making it day by day. And were we ever frightened. And God, we were hungry, and we knew what would happen if we were caught. And those who may have wanted to help us knew the punishment for aiding a Jew. Kaput—a favored words of yours during those heartbreaking years. So we never dared to get near them. We were just as afraid of them as they were of us.

A narrow path led down to the first huts. The dogs would break out into a chorus of yelping while I tiptoed across the wooden bridge. It was always night when I went there to scrounge for matches and whatever edibles were left in the basements or attics of the abandoned houses. And there were times when I went back there for no other reason than to glance at the place where I was born, the streets where my friends and I chased each other, laughed, shouted. Or just to know who I was and where I had come from. Darkness, bolted doors, a few faintly lit windows where someone had moved in, and at the least sound, I ran back as fast as my legs would carry me.

The townsfolk knew that we were hiding, though they probably didn't know how few of us were there. Those near the edge of the town, along the road skirting the forest, knew but pretended not to. Just the same, they would throw over the fence some edible food, *turnips, beets, maize, potatoes, and once in a while some bread, often hard and moldy by the time we got to it. We would come at night and search for it, crawling on four along a fence like the pigs with their snouts on the ground. The dogs would go crazy howling as soon as we would approach. But the peasants knew, and no lights ever went on.*

Why did they leave some food for us? Brotherly love? Who knows. More likely to keep us away from them. One day we ate, and then days would go by, and they would leave nothing. No rhyme, no reason.

And so we went on, at first not fully realizing the extent of the disaster that befell our town, still refusing to believe that so many lives could have been snuffed out. Like shadows at dawn, reality set in by small steps, and I finally had to admit to myself that they were gone, all of them, and only I and the twins were left to mourn them, like the few shipwrecked watching the last vestige of the ship vanishing beneath the waves.

Oh yes, the three of us. I forgot to tell you. The old man didn't make it. During one cold winter night, the wind howling, he left the hideout and never came back. Wrapped in our rags, we were asleep. Morning came, and he was nowhere in sight. We tried to find him, but snow had fallen during the night, obliterating the footprints. We should have known that something like this would happen by the way the man did some irrational things like singing to himself, carrying on a conversation with one Rivka, presumably his wife, and for all we knew, he may have gone down into the town to look for her.

You wanted to know what it must have felt seeing the Russians on the horizon. Another one of those dreams gone sour. Let me just say, there was no dancing in the street, no hugging the battle-weary soldiers coming to our rescue, no throwing flowers and kisses the way you may have seen in the movies showing the Allies liberating Paris or Rome. Far from it.

I would like to tell you about it, but now I have a visitor. Ben, a lonely man, a widower. We met on the ship bringing us to the States, and over the years we kept in touch with each other on special occasions—you know, weddings, a bar-mitzvah, unfortunately also funerals, his wife, then mine. I like Ben. A quiet man who asks for nothing more than just to be together for an hour or two to share silences. Our stories are so similar that syllables tell more than those long narratives that I tend to indulge in. Some may call it catharsis. Perhaps they are right. At any rate, while I am given to recurrent outbursts of anger—rage, you could call it—Ben never loses his equanimity. Is he made that way? Or is he seething inside with the kind of anger that is waiting to explode some day? I told him about you. He listened without interrupting, as if that too was nothing unusual. His only comment was: "I think you are crazy to even look at that mamzer." Mamzer is a Yiddish word for bastard, not exactly a nice word.

While I end this, he sits near the window and reads the newspaper.

Yours,

Nathan

CHAPTER
26

HE IS DISCOURAGED, MISS Hedberg tells me. He had a slight temperature yesterday, but it's normal now. Most of the swelling is down, and he has less pain. She was there at his bedside, and he didn't even look at her. Unshaven and unwashed, he kept staring at the ceiling the entire time. He never opened the morning paper, barely touched his food, and refused the morning medication. He hardly slept. But he read my letter. She saw the pages scattered on the table next to him, one or two having drifted to the floor. That too, she claims, is most unusual for Gerhard, the fastidious and orderly man. To all of her questions, he remained silent or barely shook his head in a gesture of wanting to be left alone.

She doesn't say so but leaves me with the impression that the man has lost interest in most things except our correspondence. Although he owes me a letter, I sit down and write to him.

Friday, the 3rd of March
Dear Gerhard,

Our postman tells me that these days you have taken a special interest in that ceiling of yours. There was a time when I used to do the same and found it utterly boring. And while you are confined to bed, let me tell you what is happening outside. This morning, the magnolia petals unfolded. The tree is right below my window. I look down at the fully opened flowers, and from above they look like pink water lilies floating in the air. Imagine, in just a few days the first blades of grass and the needle-like tips of a few crocuses have broken through the soil while dirt-crusted snow is still wedged between the raised flowerbeds. Spring it is. And just as I abhor winter, spring has always been the season of joy.

I promised to tell you how it felt leaving that cursed forest and being free. Hardly the event I anticipated it to be, but I don't mind writing about it. Perhaps this will cheer you a little. It is the least painful part of that otherwise sordid tale of mine.

It was a spring day like this one. The three of us, the twin brothers always walking a few paces behind me, approached the forest edge. The fields were still covered with snow, but some of it had melted, and mounds of black soil like ink spots on a white expanse dotted the otherwise wintry landscape. What struck my eyes was bluish smoke. Some of it came clearly from the many chimneys, but some rose from streets and alleys between the houses. It took me a few minutes to finally realize that those strange shapes within the blue *haze were military vehicles, a few of them clearly tanks and some bearing the unmistaken red star with a hammer and sickle.*

I was stunned. They were there, and we didn't hear them arrive. Deliverance came while we were wedged into our hole in the ground. Exhausted from cold and lack of food, my senses became dulled. I became apathetic and had ceased paying attention to the sounds around us. For a long time, I stood riveted to the spot in disbelief. For so long now, hunger and cold had managed to distort reality to a point of a dream-like state of only existing. Standing there in broad daylight, the fear of being seen gone, I wondered whether this was real or another hunger-induced hallucination. I shouted, at nothing in particular, just to hear the sound of my own voice, a thing I didn't dare to do for so long now. The echo reached me from somewhere in the treetops, and nothing happened. Abandoning the camouflaging underbrush, I took a few hesitant steps beyond, as if trying to prove to myself that it was safe to do so. I stood upright, abandoning my usual crouching stance, for all to see me, and nothing happened. And even then I hesitated to go down, as if the town had become a strange and forbidding place where I no longer belonged. The cursed forest had become home; it laid claim on me in more ways than I imagined. I turned to see if my companions were following me. They hadn't moved. One of them kept staring at the town, his eyes half-closed, tears running down his muddy cheeks. His brother had his arm around him and kept whispering to him. It was the first time I saw either one of them weep.

I left them and took the narrow path down. I walked slowly at first, still afraid to be visible, but soon hurried on as fast as my legs wrapped in assorted rags would allow. Down near the bridge, about to enter the street leading into town, I turned. My companions were coming down slowly, one of them visibly dragging his leg, a legacy of frostbites. I waved them on, but they didn't wave back, only kept on walking, one bracing the other.

I came upon the Russians almost suddenly. The soldiers were everywhere as if they had crept out from some underground burrows, and there were trucks, weapon carries, all kind of war machinery. I came nearer and raised my hands above my head to let them know that I was a friend of theirs who came down from my hiding, now anxious to seek their protection. But that soon seemed unnecessary. A few soldiers sat on some upturned crates, spooning something hot from their aluminum utensils. One noticed me and nudged his comrade, who looked up and waved his spoon for me to put my hands down. With his cheeks bulging, he mumbled something in Russian, of which I could only understand one word, khorosho—all right, and went on chewing. I stopped at a distance, unsure what to do or what to say.

The twins, a few paces behind me, didn't fare better. I saw them stand in front of a row of soldiers sitting on a bench against a wall, all of them eating. One of the brothers, seemingly the spokesman for both, spoke Russian and was busy explaining who they were and pointing at the forest in the distance. One of the soldiers stopped eating and shouted at him, "Pashli!"—Go away, get lost, while another broke off a chunk of bread and threw it at his feet. Starved, they threw themselves at the morsel, tearing off pieces with their hands.

It was only now, in the presence of the soldiers and the few townspeople sauntering by, that I realized what pitiful a sight the three of us must be. There we stood, emaciated, unwashed, the dirt caked into the skin, uncombed, unshaven, our legs wrapped in potato sacks stolen during our nocturnal foraging, the rags fastened by strings from knee down and over the shoes, or what was left of them. No one smiled though. Thank God, no one smiled. A small blessing. Laughter would have been more than I could have endured.

That was it, Gerhard. No cannonade, no tanks crashing through the countryside, no smiling, triumphant faces of our liberators, no outstretched arm to greet us, those miserable scraps of humanity that we had become. Just a flick of a spoon, bits of bread thrown at your feet, pashli—get lost. So much for all those speeches I was getting ready to make on coming face to face with the brave men fighting to set me free. So much for that glorious moment when the four of us, and in the end only three emaciated wrecks of human beings, would come back to claim their rights of being part of the human race.

The meek shall inherit the earth. Remember that, Gerhard? Forget it!

No tears. No welcomes. Not the Russians, not the townsfolk. To the contrary. Unwanted, we fled—unwanted, we returned.

Painful, Gerhard, but true.

I made a mistake, though. At the time, it seemed the right thing to do. One soldier, a young man, addressed me in Yiddish and wanted to know what happened. I told him. He accompanied me to the house where I lived and listened in silence as I told him what took place here. "How sad, how sad," he kept muttering and nodding his head. Same story, town after town, the same thing happened. Wherever those murderers went, they wiped out every Jewish community, burned every synagogue as if this was of greatest strategic importance.

The few townsmen on the street paid no attention to me, as if seeing a bearded, haggard, young Jew, unkempt, dressed in rags, more dead than alive was not worth looking at. Didn't they know who I was? Did the message that some of us had come back spread so quickly, and they were no longer surprised to see me? Or were they simply preoccupied with the arrival of the Russians, the new occupants, and with the Germans gone, what did the Russians have in store for them?

I turned the corner and came upon the first houses. Empty. One after the other—empty, empty. Here lived the baker, over there my uncle and his family, all empty. I slowed my steps, frightened to go on, not knowing what lay ahead, what may lurk inside those rows of shabby buildings and narrow alleys. Perhaps there were things I had failed to notice during my nightly straying there in search for food and something to wear. My knees began to tremble. I became lightheaded and sat down on the front steps of a nearby house, my Russian companion silently sitting next to me. Was it hunger, was it fear, was it the sudden realization that what awaited me within those empty dwellings was even worse than what I had imagined? Was all of this some ghostly apparition, and all I needed to do was rest awhile with my eyes closed and then open them again and find people, not many, just a few, a child, an old man, anyone I could speak to, hear my own voice, hear their voices, put a lie to that emptiness? I opened my eyes. The empty ghetto was there, unchanged, only blurred now, and I closed my eyes again and let the tears run freely.

We went toward the house where I lived, my footsteps muffled by the burlap wrapped around my feet. How the deserted ghetto and I resembled each other. Haggard, shabby, unkempt, an emptiness yawning back at me with its windows, many of the panes missing.

I reached my house, just a hut. The door was closed, and I knocked. An older man, a peasant came out. I told him who I was and that this used to be our hut. While I spoke, his eyes were riveted to the gun the Russian toted across his chest, the kind with a disc-like magazine clip—they called it a dyekterova or avtomat or something. The man's face turned ashen. He shot out of the house and disappeared around the corner. The word must have gotten around that the Jews had come back with the Russians in tow to chase the good folks out of their homes, and God knows what other idiotic nonsense.

You should have seen the inside of the house—bare walls and

bare floors. Hardly anything left. While we were up there in the forest, less than a couple of kilometers away, within shouting distance, you could say, the townspeople, those good, pious Christians, made off with what was of use to them, another name for looting.

I stepped over the threshold. My hand reached toward the mezuzah, that holy emblem attached to the door post as you enter. It was gone; someone ripped it off. Only a dark spot now in the otherwise sun-bleached wood. You must have seen these while sauntering through the ghetto. The main room, that single room where we lived, ate, quarreled, sang on the Sabbath, had been plundered. All of the furnishings were gone except for a bench, a few chairs, the table, a pallet in the corner—someone must have been living there during my absence. Perhaps it was that man who just left. The whitewashed earthen stove was still warm. The stove plate with its rings in the center was rusty now, the wall and ceiling soot-stained. Mama's domain. Here she spent a good part of the day squatting in front of the oven door and blowing at the kindling, getting short of breath, coughing, wheezing like bellows, her thin chest heaving.

My eyes went to the floor, once her pride. In a flash, it all came back—the Friday afternoon ritual of scrubbing, the brush with hard bristles, Mama on her knees, spilling soapy water and then wiping it with an old piece of burlap, her hands red and chafed. Those same coarse hands that at other times would rinse another piece of cloth to place on my forehead to take away the fever. It was all there, still clinging to the air and to my wanting to hear the sound of scrubbing of the wooden boards, the hissing of the many pots splashing on the hot stove plate, the air redolent of gray soap and the Sabbath bread baking in the oven. This and a barrage of a thousand other images became compressed into a single flash of remembering as I stood there in the middle of the room, not knowing what to do.

And now there were cobwebs stretched over the corners of the windowpanes. Mama hated cobwebs. And there in the corner between the stove and the bench, the one thing so painfully familiar— the broom with worn-down bristles and the blackened handle. There it stood like a sentinel of the creaking floorboards, unswept, stained now, mud-caked. It was all gone, the candle holders, Mama's pots hanging on the wall, a whole array of them, copper and cast iron, like precious medals displayed on the wall above the stove, each one a trophy to attest to her bravery against the onslaught of many hungry days, all of them taken away, the dust-free imprints still visible.

Only the attic was spared the plunderer's greed. Not much to plunder there—only a box with old books, Hebrew, Yiddish, the pages eared and brown. Papa smoked, and he would turn the pages with his tobacco-stained fingers. An old picture album, the spine torn off and many pages loose and scattered between the floor rafters. I bent down to pick them up. Sepia brown eyes were staring back at me, telling me to leave them alone for the time being—too dark up here to look at them.

I entered the store. The shelves had been taken down and used to fashion two crudely made bedsteads and boards. Here stood once

Reb Klein, my father, the seller of shoes, the haggler, the man who started as a cobbler with his singular love for his handmade shoes and utter contempt for those made by a machine in some big city and only God knew by what unclean hands.

How slow and painful that first day of coming home. How painful noticing the things missing, things around me, irrelevant all my life and now so meaningful. The familiar creaking of a door, the earthy pungency of packed dirt in the entranceway, the rancid smell of stale water in a barrel, the scent of leather from my phylacteries. Of all the things to do, I reached for the broom and began sweeping the floor just to be doing something. I found myself gripping the handle, greasy and sweat-stained, Mama's private weapon against dust and cockroaches. Her hands were on it, and so were the hands of my sisters and brother. And often mine too. We swept with it, used it as a weapon against each other's wrath or to just stand there in the middle of the room and dream while pretending to do something useful. The broom, the knobby and crooked handle, my pitiful heirloom, a link to the past now, their hands and now mine touching it. Swish, swish, I went long after there was nothing left to sweep away. Silly thing to do after returning home to a place that was no longer home, a place no longer worth coming back to, and I standing there no longer the boy, the loving and loved young boy of just a few months ago. An old man I had turned into, a boy dressed in tatters, clutching the handle of an old, grime-crusted broom handle. I held on to it out of sense of kinship.

And so I spent my first night at home, the stove warm, a fire, and the crackling of dried logs that were left there stashed against the eaves. I slept on a straw mattress, waking up with a start to unfamiliar sounds only to go back to sleep in the realization that I was safe now. It was during the night that the emptiness filled with strange sounds, the creaking of rafters, the scurrying of mice, someone breathing heavily, sleep-murmuring, restlessly turning on a straw mattress, all emanating from a corner near the stove where a bed stood a long time ago.

How capricious the mind. Like a sentinel at the gate of memories, it selects what to remember and what to forget, even if it is only for the time being. Nearly fifty years now, and I still remember vividly the next day of sitting on the stoop of our hut, my feet bare, having at last discarded the sackcloth bindings, sitting there and savoring the taste of that first gulp of milk and of the freshly baked bread someone with a trace of heart had left at the door, my trembling hands, my emaciated fingers tearing off big chunks and wolfing them down, forgetting for a while that the hut and the other dwellings around me were one vast graveyard. My first meal among the tombstones.

But enough of this.

I just opened the window. A whiff of warm air brushed against my face. It's spring. There is no mistake. So hurry up, my friend, before the bench grows cold again.

Nathan

CHAPTER
27

I CAN WALK NOW. I drag my left leg, but taking mincing steps, I can conceal my limp. I can walk over to the window, open it, and leaning against the windowsill, I can look down. The gardener, my assiduous leaf gatherer during the season of wilt, is there again. His small cart is filled with potted flowers. Envious, I watch the man as he places individual pots along the edges and then, kneeling on the soft flowerbed, plants them in the ground. Primroses, daisies, splashes of color, young plantings like freshly scrubbed children colorfully dressed in their Sunday best. If only I could get back to my apartment, no garden there, only a small porch, all the plants potted and cared for by my next-door neighbor.

A small draft tells me that someone has opened the door. She enters with bouncy steps, a green scarf around her neck, a miniature white rose pinned to her lapel.

"Happy Saint Patrick's Day, and a top o' the mornin' to ye," she announces, clearly pleased with her Irish brogue. It still carries the Swedish lilt. "And what are we looking at so intently down there in the garden?"

"Spring, Miss Hedberg, flowers, the air. I can walk now. Look." I show her how well I can shift my weight and take a step.

"Ja, ja, Mr. Klein. You and that friend of yours, restless the both of you. He too keeps looking out of the window."

"Is he ready to walk now?"

"Any day now. You mustn't rush things, you know."

"A cane, Miss Hedberg, an ordinary cane." I nod at the metallic one with a tripod at the end. "A walking stick, none of this contraption. Just an ordinary walking cane."

"And what is the occasion, if you don't mind my asking?" She quizzically raises her eyebrows.

"And another thing, Miss Hedberg, for once would you mind not walking behind me with your arms protectively stretched out like wings?"

"Ja, ja." She nods her head. "And so you wish to go for a walk all by yourself—a rendezvous, I see. And may I be informed when it is about to take place?"

There is a tinge of sarcasm in her voice. There has been more of it recently. Could she be resentful that now, strength returning to my limbs, I'm no longer in need of her? But a while later, she comes back carrying several canes, the curved handles draped over her forearm.

"There, this one ought to do." She makes me stand straight while she fits one to my height. "There, just the right size." She steps back and watches me stand unaided. Pleased, she smiles to herself. "Now, take a few steps and do it very slowly. Ja, Mr. Klein, you are doing fine, just fine."

He is in the garden. I see him walk slowly toward the bench. He stops and using his woolen gloves wipes the slats. He turns slowly before letting himself down and finally leans back, stretching his leg, raising the leg so miraculously saved and placing it on top of the wooden prosthesis. I watch him, this time with the kind of gladness one feels at the sight of a train pulling into the station and an old friend stepping down. Next to me is the desk with a drawer full of letters bridging the span of time between my first recognition of the man and the one sitting there, his leg miraculously saved. Strange, the coincidence of time. Then too, fifty years ago, between autumn and spring when he lost his Esta and I lost all those that I once loved.

Ah, what letters they are. I scan some of them, insulting, begging, cajoling, letters of hope and letters of despair. Lengthy letters in which I, Nathan, bared my soul to the man I once feared and hated, and in the end went on to bolster his failing spirit. Letters to me from a man who once hated me with a passion that knew no bounds and is now searching my companionship and forgiveness.

How invisible those bonds have grown since that first letter of mine in which I likened him to a nightmare come alive. I open the window and stand there watching him open the topmost button of his winter coat. Our eyes meet, and for a while we keep staring at each other. He waves at me. I see him reach back for the cane he has hooked over the back of the bench, and I wave back, bidding him to stay where he is, letting him know that I'm on my way to see him. He smiles and puts the cane back.

It's a slow walk. Part of me wishing to hurry, to meet the man who in a short span of time of confiding has transformed from an arrogant Nazi officer to an old man full of remorse, a man grappling with the past, as I am with mine. I have to rein myself in to walk slowly, showing as little infirmity as possible and none of the stoop of the fearful.

Mercifully, they built a gradually sloping ramp for those unable to walk the steps. I look at him and see his gaze following each step of mine. I stand before him. He too stands now and takes my hand in both of his and nods at the bench. He seems to be as wanting for words, as I am, and I wonder if he too has a lump in his throat.

I suddenly become aware that this stooped, round-backed, and round-shouldered man is nearly a head shorter than I am. This cannot be. I silently shake my head. Have I grown since I was the seventeen-year-old, frightened adolescent standing on trembling legs before the man? A giant he seemed then. Was it his height, or was it his power that so towered over me? Or was it fear as I stood and watched him lift his riding crop and bring it to my forehead?

My young giant of a lifetime ago turned into an aged dwarf.

We sit down, and I can feel his shoulder close to mine, and I too drape the handle of my cane over the back of the bench. At close distance, his face is angular, too much flesh hanging loosely, as if the bones were too small to accommodate it. His light eyes are surrounded by red-rimmed eyelids. Brown patches dot his forehead like an archipelago of dark islands on otherwise fair but wrinkled skin. Thin-lipped, he smiles at me, and I try to read in it more than what may simply be embarrassment of finally meeting each other eye to eye. He fidgets with his gloves, uncertain whether to put them on or leave them off, and I now see purple blotches on the back of his wrist, a legacy of intravenous fluid they must have given him in the hospital. I know; I had the same spots during my encounter with the doctors right after the stroke. Ugly tattoos and constant reminders of the fragility of our body at our ages.

"Well." He clears his throat. "We finally meet." His voice too is smaller than I suspected, and cracked. It is the voice of a feeble, bedridden man for so many months now.

"Primroses." He breaks the silence and nods at the freshly

planted floral display right next to our bench. "My favored flowers, and those too." He nods again at another spray of yellow and white snapdragons planted along the other side of the path.

"Never had much luck with those," I say, referring to a freshly planted clump of cyclamen. "Something or other always feeds on them, making big holes in the leaves."

"I like tulips," he says.

"They wilt too soon, and after the petals fall, what is left are ugly, yellowing stems," I reply, and he nods in agreement.

And we sit again, silently staring ahead of us. I would like to say more, certainly not that silly talk of two old men sitting on a bench and finding nothing else to do than chitchat about flowers. There was so much pain, so much of everything in those letters, so much revealing of our innermost to just sit here and talk of primroses and cyclamen. But those were letters, I realize, and in these we used a different language than simple, everyday words. And I suddenly realize that I need to learn to speak to him in a language as yet foreign to me.

Miss Hedberg's face suddenly appears in my window and then vanishes again. In that quick interval, I catch her gaze. She is somber, seemingly unsure if the two us are ready to sit there side by side. Like a mama seeing for the first time her small charge let go of her hand and plunge into the melee of playmates in the sandbox.

"Well, Nathan, I hope you don't mind if I call you Nathan,"

he finally speaks up, his voice firmer now, as if he has managed to gather additional strength. "Now that we're sitting next to each other, do you still see the two of me, or is it one at last?"

"Right now, only one. But you know, Gerhard, that other one has a nasty habit of suddenly popping up like ducks in a shooting gallery. But now I see only one."

"Ah yes, you are not the only one who is trying to get rid of that other one." Gerhard shakes his head. "He too hounds me, for different reasons though. In time, Nathan, you might forget him, and I pray that you do. But I cannot. Whatever you remember of him, my friend, I was that man, and I vividly recall every breath and every step he took."

"You know what, Gerhard? Each time you and I talk about the past, I keep thinking of a television program I once watched, one of those travelogues. There was one scene I can never forget. It was somewhere in the Middle East, but it could have been North Africa. It was a long procession of men, mostly middle-aged, and they filled the street from curb to curb. They carried whips, those cat-o'-nine-tails kind, and naked from the waist up, they kept whipping their bloodied backs. Self-flagellation, they call it. Isn't that what we two are doing to ourselves? Look around us, Gerhard. Spring, the bees are humming, the sun is trying to break through, and here we sit, the two of us, two men, sharing between us one pair of good legs."

"One pair of good legs." He chuckled. "I like that—one pair

of good legs between the two of us." He smiled broadly, revealing his dentures, the teeth way too large and regular for a man with thin lips and a slack-set and somewhat sagging chin.

"And have you noticed our Miss Hedberg briefly showing her face in the window?" I nodded at the still-open window. "She was there a short while ago and disappeared."

"A short while ago, did you say?" he retorts. "That woman was watching me all morning, and realizing that I finally intended to get up and go out—never mind what the doctor's orders were—she was as agitated as a mother seeing her daughter stepping out on her first date."

"Do you suppose she is still watching us?"

"Wouldn't be surprised to see her sauntering by. And by the way, it was Miss Hedberg, more than all the doctors with all that fancy surgery and whatnot, who saved my leg. She was there at my bedside when I needed her most. 'Just a few more days, and you'll be all well.' She would bend over to fix my pillow, her partly unbuttoned shirt revealing a deep cleavage between her generous breasts, and that perfume of hers ..."

"Lavender."

"That's right, lavender. Intoxicating at times. Takes you away from whatever ails you at the moment, no? Or should a man my age no longer notice these things?"

He smiles again, and I'm not sure if it's at the recollection of Miss Hedberg's breasts against his face or at the sun just breaking through the clouds and flooding the garden with bright light.

"To hell with age," I reply. "It wasn't all that easy to lie there on my back on one of those exercise couches, and our Miss Hedberg pulling up the bed sheet all the way up to my private parts, grasping my thigh, her fingers right next to my you-know-what, while at the same time I was trying to listen to her instructions on how to raise and lower my legs and so forth."

Our conversation drifts back to primroses and cyclamens, but this time we also touch on our visitors. We speak of automobiles, and I learn of his fondness of cars. I tell him about my son, Robert, and his attractive young wife. He is surprised to hear that she was my daughter-in-law, having noticed her on a few occasions stepping out of a Jaguar in the parking lot and wondering who was so lucky to have such a beautiful visitor. I ask him about his visitors, and he is dismissive.

"There is, of course, my uncle's family," he speaks reluctantly. "The old bookworm died. Fell off the ladder reaching for some ancient tome. But there are the two sons of his, both married with lots of children. Cousins we are, but they are much younger, and we seem to have lived on two different planets. The past, my past is to them one of those blank pages of history in which they have no interest whatever. I tried to speak of some of the things that happened during the war, our tragedies, the tragedies of others. Big yawns. One of the little ones wanted to know if this was about the, 'Civil War, you know, the freeing of the slaves, you know.'

"My uncle, may his soul rest in peace, and many of his friends belonged to the German Cultural Society, German bookstores, spoke German, and insisted that German was spoken at home. While Germany cities were being reduced to rubble, they spent the war years comfortably in their homes here in the United States. Remember what you wrote to me in one of your letters? Men will remember only what they choose to remember and forget what they wish to forget."

"Did I write that? I don't remember."

"You certainly did."

"Must have been someone else who wrote that."

"It couldn't have been someone else. You were the only one who wrote to me."

"And you kept all those letters?"

"I certainly did. I remember every word. Kept reading some of them again and again. Clipped them together and put them into a special folder. And you?"

"Stashed them into a drawer, one on top of the other, the most recent one on top. No, I'm afraid I lack your sense of order and neatness. Speaking of letters, I never did thank you for that fine ivory letter opener."

"You liked it?"

"I did. Kept fingering the smooth ivory. Where did you get

it? Don't tell me you got it somewhere during the war. I don't want to know."

"You mean plunder?" He glances at me from the corner of his eyes with a smirk on his thin lips. "Nathan, my friend, that other Gerhard doesn't just pop up, the way you described it awhile ago. It seems you keep looking for him. They have a neat saying, 'Forever looking under the rug to find the dirt.' But if you must know, I obtained it from a Jew. In fact, it was a Jewess. And was she ever gorgeous—raven-black hair and green eyes. She owned an antique shop right downtown in Jerusalem. Mesmerized by her looks, I hardly saw it or listened to her telling me how old it was and where it came from. She spoke English with a trace of Dutch."

"And she reminded you of ..."

"No, no." He shakes his head. "If anything, she kept displaying her wedding band to remind me that she was a married woman, and I was old enough to be her father. How about those two men, the twins who made it to freedom, ever heard from them?"

"Not a word. They went their own way without as much as a handshake or a good-bye. We simply couldn't wait to part from one another, We had nothing in common before it all happened, and even less once we found ourselves having to share a hole in the ground. A cesspool, filth, hunger, debasement, envy of the man dressed in a warmer coat than your own, wearing solid boots instead of my flimsy shoes, coming back from our nightly foray and seeing the other man stuffing his mouth with something edible, too dark to see what it was—no, Gerhard, this was not the stuff to bring people together."

"I suppose they too had lost their family?"

"We all had lost our families, and in that sense, we were all devastated. I suppose, looking at the men crouching over the fire or huddled in a dugout beneath the root of a fallen tree, and knowing that you're not alone with that heartache of yours made it easier to endure. But all that lofty stuff about comradeship forged by common danger, sharing your last morsel of food in a dugout and so forth is so much nonsense written by romantic writers who never smelled gunpowder or the stench of rotting wounds. The twins, they could have been a single human being cleaved in two, thinking the same way, acting the same way, even praying the same way and at the same time. They needed no one else."

Heavy clouds conceal the sun, and a raw breeze drifts across the garden. Gerhard raises the collar of his winter overcoat and stashes his hands into the pockets. I see him shudder and grimace as he flexes his one good leg.

"Sorry, Nathan, but we mustn't overdo this. Our guardian angel will disapprove. She has some temper, or haven't you noticed?"

We part. Leaving the path and entering the ramp, I stop and

watch him go in the opposite direction toward his pavilion. He walks with a foot-dragging limp, twisting his torso with each step. Before disappearing around the bend, he too stops, turns, and waves, seemingly aware that I am watching him.

CHAPTER
28

A RESTLESS SLEEPER MOST OF the time, I'm wide awake at dawn and watch the sun come up, the first rays spreading over the rooftops and the uppermost branches of the trees. My ear attuned to the usual morning sounds, I wait to hear footsteps on the gravely path below the window. I welcome the arrival of the day shift and then the food, followed by Miss Hedberg. And there is now the anticipation of Gerhard making his appearance. He will be there, the way he was these last few days, wearing the same winter overcoat. He too has a ritual now. He will sit down on his bench, no longer exactly in the middle as was his habit in the past; instead he will sit offside, as if making room for me to sit near him. He will take off his gloves, look at his hands as if making sure that they are there, loosen the top button of his coat, loosen his collar with his customary circular motion of his fingers inside, and only then will he turn his head to gaze at the window in anticipation of my making an appearance. He has gotten into the habit of wearing a visored cloth cap, and at the sight of me, he touches the visor with the tip of his fingers. Damn, if it doesn't look like a military salute. I pretend not to notice it.

A sense of order has replaced the randomness of my daily routine. I can walk. I can look down at things from the full height of me, no longer from the vantage of a wheelchair. I can grasp things with my left hand, though clumsily, I still keep dropping things. I can squeeze the toothpaste, wield a fork and knife at the same time, and I can brace myself with both arms. The disobedient left side of me has returned like a prodigal son, content now to be back and trying to make amends.

It's time to go home, to my desk, my books, my window with a view of the skyline in the distance, and the newspaper stand around the corner. I look forward to the early morning hours at home and, with the window ajar, hearing the clanging of the garbage truck, followed by the bedlam of the morning traffic. And around midmorning come the tap, tap of small feet as the kindergarten tots are being led to the park. Children. I cannot wait to see them walking, arms swinging, hop-skipping, jostling one another. Most of my neighbors and friends are old. Most are mirrors of myself—stooped, walking with a shuffle, their faces reflecting the toll that time takes on all of us. The sight of children, red-cheeked and giggling, gladdens the eye.

We meet, Gerhard and I. He's first to arrive to our daily rendezvous, although no one set such rules of our conduct. We never wrote to each other again, even on days when there was rain or a gusty wind. I simply look down and know that on days like this he will stay inside.

And there are now days when we speak, but our words seem to lack the intensity of our letter writing. Bench companions, bird watchers, we follow with our eyes the flight of birds on their way back to nest here again. Gerhard, with his head raised to the sky, his eyes half-closed, as if his face were a moving radar antenna, follows the path of the sun as it winds its way between the clouds. These last few days, we have little to say to each other, and when we speak, the flow of words is constrained, as if all that each of us had to say to the other has already been accomplished.

Was it easier for me to speak about myself in those letters to the man who was only a figment of my imagination at the time of my writing? Was I writing my first letter to the same Gerhard that I wrote the last letter to? Was I shifting my Gerhards to match my changing perceptions of him like a card player discarding the cards he didn't like, taking new ones from the deck to suit his hand?

Sitting next to him, I'm constrained to one Gerhard only. He is here. I can see him, touch him, hear his voice—an old man, a cripple. He taps his artificial leg with his cane. Hollow inside, he makes it sound like a bongo drum. A man sniffling, squinting his eyes, running his finger along the inside of his collar in that old gesture of his, the pedantic, claustrophobic, acrophobic, forgiveness-seeking man, and at times, a bit petulant and irritating. I can no longer shift him back and forth like a weaver his shuttle. I try hard to conjure up that young Nazi-saluting thug, but I find him more distant now, and I have to settle on the man sitting beside me.

Or could our letter writing have been a flash, a single moment in our lives, one brought about by despair, our illness underscoring the frailty of our existence, and the threat that these may be our last days? Did we, the two old men, bare ourselves in a last-ditch attempt to tell things we had harbored a lifetime with no one willing to listen? Were these the proverbial swan songs of our lives? And having finished with the last refrain, our songs have come to an end?

We go on sitting next to each other like hibernating porcupines—close enough to keep warm but not all that close to hurt one another with their quills. And occasionally we do speak. My old habit of thinking that my brain, in order to function, needs the sound of my voice in the way an engine needs fuel. Gerhard listens, his face directed to the sun, his eyes closed, the glasses pushed way up over his forehead. He listens, and his head bobs up and down, or he shakes it slowly from side to side when disagreeing. After a while, I grow tired speaking, perhaps lulled by the sound of my own voice, and closed-eyed,

I too follow the sun and let the warmth caress my face. Haven't done this for a long time. Strangely enough, I feel at peace sitting close to the man I once so feared and detested—more at ease than I did while writing those letters to him.

And there are other times when we sit silently and only once in a while touch upon the past, but with gloved hands and sunglasses to shield our eyes from the bright sun and from having to gaze at each other. Once in a while, our eyes wander to a window just opened and see another face lifted to the sky. Old faces most of them, a sprinkle of young ones, but even these have the pallor of illness etched on them, a furtive look, retiring, almost afraid to be seen there, as if sunshine was reserved only for the healthy and the young.

We have gotten into the habit of walking up and down the path, our steps guarded, our canes on the outside to give us more room to walk close to each other. Even our limps have become synchronous. Gerhard has the habit of stopping each time he has some comment to make or to doff his hat to other residents passing by. Annoyed, I continue, and he hurries with his wobbly gait to catch up with me. Short of breath, he tells me who they were and what ailed them. Damned habit of his of referring to them as "that old Italian man that just passed by" or "the German woman in the wheelchair." Back in my neighborhood, it was customary to refer to others by their country of origin, but it somehow rankles when he does it.

CHAPTER
29

It is another morning, the air crisp and the sun bright, too dazzling bright for my mood.

"Well, shall we go for a walk, or are you too tired?" I ask him.

"And sit here on the bench on a beautiful spring day like this?" Gerhard replies while he unbuttons his coat and loosens the shawl around his neck.

It's time to tell him, I feel. Miss Hedberg has guessed it for some time, already seeing me drop things more clumsily than ever. The smirk on her face would tell me that she knew I could do better if only I wanted to. She knew that I was pretending to be clumsy, but there was no need to. And we both knew it was time to go home.

"Soon I'll be leaving here, Gerhard," I tell him at last.

He doesn't seem surprised and continues with his rocking gait, his artificial leg dragging slightly behind.

"I suspected it." He stops and nods. "How soon?"

"Tomorrow."

For a long while, we walk on silently as if I haven't mentioned my leaving or he hasn't heard me. "That soon?" He finally breaks the silence, his voice barely above a whisper. He doesn't raise his head, only continues staring at the pebbly path.

I too remain silent, not wanting to elaborate on what seems to be upsetting him deeply.

"How long have you known?" he asks after a long pause.

"About a week."

"And you didn't say a word?"

"I thought it would make you sad."

He nods and tugs at his shirt collar again.

"And you, Gerhard, how long will they keep you here?"

"Oh, I can leave whenever I want to," he says, trying to make it sound casual.

"And so you stayed here for my sake?"

"For your sake, Nathan, for my sake—who knows? Does it really matter?" Gerhard shrugs and resumes walking.

"Are you all packed?" he asks me.

I nod and slow down and reach up to break off a small sprig of lilac, the petals about to open. We walk on while I twirl the stem between my fingers.

"And where will you go from here?" he asks.

"Back to my apartment. And you, Gerhard?"

"Same thing. Back to my apartment. Will I see you after we leave here?" he says now, his face drawn and his brows knitted.

"Sure," I say, trying to reassure him. "There is a nice place right around the corner from where I live. A small park with a water fountain, a few benches to sit on and feed the pigeons, or just sit. The subway is just—"

"What about rain and all that?" He stops me in midsentence.

"Nothing to it, Gerhard. Right across the street from the park, they have a coffee shop. A real, your-style *Kaffeehouse*. You can get your damned *Wiener Kaffee mit Schlagsahne* there, the whip cream mounded and spilling over the rim. On a sunny day, they have a few tables on the sidewalk shielded by an awning. Or if the weather is really bad, you can sit inside by one of those large picture windows, and you can watch the people walking by."

"You see, Nathan. We ... how shall I say it ... we sort of need one another."

"How's that?"

"Well, it's hard to explain. You see ..." He halts again and places his hand on my elbow to make sure that I too stop. "You see, I'm a man who needs someone to explain myself to, and you are ... well, it hurts, it hurts a lot to have no one to share the past with." He is silent after that, as if regretting what he said, but soon he raises his head again.

"Did I tell you about the time I walked by an antique store, and my eye was caught by a small item in the window?" he says. "A gauge it was, one of those carving tools with an ornate wooden handle. What drew my attention to it was the wood. You see, I know wood by now, and this was the finest, the kind of hardwood used for making violin parts. I went inside just to look at it. I brushed away the dust, and near the rim was some carving, clearly handmade. And there were initials carved in: AA. You realize what that could be?"

"No, tell me."

"AA. Now, mind you, I cannot be sure, but AA could stand for Andrea Amati, the great Amati, the founder of the school of violin makers in …"

I try to listen to his bubbly enthusiasm about the old master, the founder of an entire dynasty of violin makers.

"And wouldn't it be a strange coincidence," he says," if the master's own tools found their way to New York, to sit there in the corner of some obscure antique shop, right next to some oil lamp used by a miner in the Old West, and wouldn't it be …"

After a while, I lose the trend of his narrative as he goes on about Cremona in the sixteenth century and about the Amati progeny and how they maintained the old tradition of making violins and other string instruments.

I hand him the sprig of fragrant lilac. He takes it and without looking at it puts the stem into the buttonhole of his coat, and we walk on.